THE MEMORY CHILD

THE MEMORY CHILD

Steena Holmes

Published by

LAKE UNION
PUBLISHING

Published by Lake Union Publishing, Seattle

www.apub.com

Amazon, the Amazon logo, and Lake Union Publishing are trademarks of Amazon. com, Inc., or its affiliates.

ISBN-13: 9781477818428

ISBN-10: 1477818421

Library of Congress Control Number: 2013917820

Printed in the United States of America

A mother's love is patient and forgiving

when all others are forsaking,

it never fails or falters,

even though the heart is breaking.

—Helen Rice

CHAPTER ONE

Diane

Present–February

This was a perfect moment. In the silence, with the hint of dawn peeking through the curtains, where promises of a better day were offered.

I stared down at the twinkling blue eyes of my sweet darling baby and knew hope for the first time in a long, long time. Grace was everything I didn't deserve and everything I longed for. Just one look at her bow-shaped lips, wispy blond hair, and sweeping eyelashes and I knew, from the moment I first saw her, that I could never go back to the way I used to be.

"I'm so sorry I have to leave you," I whispered, not wanting to wake her. We had a rough night and at least one of us deserved some rest.

I drew my newborn daughter close and breathed in the smell of fresh baby powder. To think I never wanted this experience, to never feel the slight weight of my child in my arms, to never see the twinkle in her eyes as she stared up at me and recognized me for who I was. Her mother. The thought that I never wanted to be a mother . . . how selfish could I have been? Everything I'd ever worried about became insignificant the moment I held her.

Grace's lashes fluttered for a few moments before resting on her cheeks. I could have stood there for hours and held her while she slept, but instead, I gently placed her down in the bassinet and stepped away, careful to keep my steps light.

What was I thinking? To leave her after only one month? I wasn't ready. She wasn't ready. My heart splintered into tiny cracks with each step I took.

What kind of a mother was I? I was abandoning my child for my career. I thought I could do it, that it wouldn't be difficult for me, that like many others, I could find a way to juggle motherhood with my profession.

What if I'd made a mistake?

"Are we ready?"

My breath caught as Nina's voice carried up the stairs. I gently closed Grace's bedroom door. Nina, our nanny/housekeeper/some-times jailer, stood at the bottom. She held my travel mug in one hand and brown leather messenger bag in the other.

Was I ready? Not really. This was the hardest thing I'd ever had to do in my life.

Nina's face softened as she smiled. I liked to call her the grey dragon on my bad days. On my good days, she was my best friend. I'm not sure what I would have done without her.

"Does it ever get easier?" I reached for the coffee, took a sip, then grimaced. "Come on, Nina, not today of all days. Didn't you get any of the French vanilla creamer I asked you to pick up?"

There was a look on Nina's face that I wasn't too sure about. Pity, maybe?

I didn't care. In the past three months since Nina first came to help while I was on bed rest, she'd been trying to get me to eliminate sugar from my diet.

"It'll get easier. I promise." Nina reached out and touched the sleeve on my jacket. "I need you to trust me. We talked about this, remember? One step at a time. Just like changing your diet to lessen the effects of your medication."

I took a deep breath and straightened my jacket before smoothing out the one black pencil skirt I could still fit into.

"I'm not sure this is a step I can take today." I knew I should, that was normal for most mothers to head back to work so soon after giving birth, but I'm not most mothers. I'm Diane Wright, CEO of HK Solutions, a cutting-edge firm that creates software for the blind. I needed to snap out of it but my feet were rooted to the floor as if cemented there. I listened for a sound, any sound, to come out of Grace's room. All it would take was a small sigh, the beginning of a cry, and I would cancel everything and stay home.

"Just come with me into the kitchen. Grace will be fine." Nina walked ahead of me and I followed obediently.

"Do you need my monitor, or do you have yours?" As insane as it sounded, I had a deathly fear that something was going to happen to Grace if I wasn't there. She could cough and ended up choking, or smother in her blanket, or even . . .

"Everything's going to be okay." Nina gave me a motherly smile.

"I'm sorry, I know I'm being . . ." What was the word I was trying to find? Overprotective? Distrusting? Smothering?

"Perfectly normal. You have a busy day today, full of appointments and a new schedule to get used to. Let's concentrate on that, shall we? Everything else will be fine." Nina held open the fridge door and pulled out the creamer. "Here, maybe a gradual withdrawal will be easier for you to handle."

"I told you so," I muttered beneath my breath.

"Don't be like that. We've had this talk. You were the one who asked me to hold you accountable." Nina glared at me. I glared back.

"We also talked about how I wasn't willing to give up my coffees."

"You don't seem to be willing to give up much when push comes to shove," Nina mumbled.

I only shrugged.

Losing the baby weight wasn't as easy as I thought it would have been, and while I was desperate to make it into my pre-baby clothing before Brian came home from opening the London office, I also had to be realistic. I loved food. I always have. It was one of Brian's and my passions. But I worked hard to make sure it didn't show on my body, too.

Brian had left the country just before I went into labor and wasn't scheduled to return for another week or so. I know it must have killed him not to be there, but everything had happened so fast that by the time his flight arrived in London, she'd already been born. I e-mailed him videos and photos of Grace daily but made sure not to include any full-length images of myself. Not until the pudge around my waistline was gone.

"Are you ready for today?" Nina smoothed her sweater over her pants.

Since I've known Nina, I've always been home. She came on board as my nurse when I went on bed rest two months before Grace was due. I had some complications, and since Brian had to travel to London at the same time, we hired a nurse to stay with me. Mainly for Brian's peace of mind. Nina worked out so well that we asked her to stay on board as nanny until I felt capable enough to do it on my own. Plus we were all to travel to London and stay with Brian for a bit, since I had some time off.

Except that part of the plan hadn't worked out yet.

"Am I ready for today? Not really. I have a feeling Walter won't accept my conditions and it'll be a struggle. Knowing him, he'll devise a strategy to have me come in every day."

Nina's lips quirked. "Really? I thought for sure he was the one telling you to stay home."

"He's just saying that. I can tell he needs me there." My relationship with Walter was a special one. Not only was he my boss, but he was like a father to me. There wasn't anything I wouldn't do for him. Anything.

"Or maybe you're just using that as an excuse? Remember, I'm here if you need me." Nina laid her hand on my arm and smiled. She really was pretty. She'd been a nurse for years, and it amazed me that she would stay by my side when she could go back to her previous job in a hospital.

"Thank you. I'm not exactly sure when I'll be back." I checked my watch and sighed. I needed to go. "I'll try to be home as early as possible. Brian might call and I don't want to miss him again. I love reading his cards and letters, but they just aren't the same. I need to hear his voice."

"If anyone calls, I'll be sure to take a detailed message." Nina stood there, calm and composed, while inside I felt like I was being torn into two. I almost hated her in that moment. She was able to stay home with my daughter while I had to go to a job I wasn't even sure I wanted anymore.

Funny how having a child changed things so drastically. Once upon a time, I used to know what my focus was, where I wanted to be in life. Having children was never part of the plan. But the moment I held Grace, all that disappeared. I'd been unprepared for the changes having a baby meant, and still it didn't seem real. Grace was only a few months old and already I was heading back into work? Where were my priorities? Why couldn't I just stay home and take care of my daughter? It was like I was being split into two different personalities.

The doorbell rang and in that moment, I was tempted to rush back upstairs, sit in the rocker, and be content to watch my daughter all day long.

The sound of heels tapping on the hardwood floors stopped me, though. The soft cadence of voices when Nina answered the door filtered through the hallway.

"Mandy, come on in. She's almost ready to go."

"Amanda?" Seeing her was a jolt. She was a reminder that I had commitments to keep; responsibilities that didn't stop just because I gave birth to the most precious thing in my life. Brian says that I am the master of masks. If so, then it was time to don a mask I wasn't sure I wanted to wear anymore. I pushed back my shoulders, took a deep breath, and began the process of compartmentalizing my life. It was the only way I'd be able to get through today. I placed my briefcase down on the entranceway table and faced my assistant. Her coming to my home, while I was on my way to work, didn't make sense.

A tentative smile grew on Amanda's lips and stayed there while I just stared. She looked . . . different. Older, maybe?

"Did you cut your hair? And lose weight?"

She didn't say anything.

"Why are you here?" Never, in the three years that we'd worked together, had Amanda come to my home uninvited.

I'd hired timid little Amanda Bell to be my new assistant when I first received the promotion to vice president at HK Solutions a few years ago. The idea of molding an assistant to suit my needs rather than retraining one seemed appealing. Amanda had been straight out of college but had the highest grades in the class. Her work ethic proved it, even though, at the time, her wardrobe did not.

It took almost a year for Amanda to realize she needed to dress the part before she could command the attention and respect from others in the office. Gone was the little girl who wore loafers and cardigans into work each day. In her place rose a woman of stature, in pencil skirts, blouses, and heels. For her birthday last year, I'd even gifted her with a pearl necklace and earrings, proud of the woman she'd become.

But that still didn't excuse her adding chaperone to her list of duties.

The glance between Nina and Amanda didn't go unnoticed.

"Mandy wanted to help make your first day back as stress-free as possible," Nina answered.

Really? "Did Walter send you to be my chauffeur?"

Amanda shrugged, and in that moment, I realized I was missing a bigger picture.

"I do not need to be babysat." I fished my keys out of my purse, grabbed my bag, and walked past both women with my head held high.

"Considering you're going to be late now to work"—I stopped just as I reached the door—"you might as well pick up some coffee for us both since we'll be spending the morning together, and be sure to buy enough muffins for everyone in the office."

My hand trembled as I gripped the doorknob and pulled it open. I couldn't help myself from glancing over my shoulder and up the stairs. All I needed was a small cry, a whimper, anything to prove that being a mother was more important than being a businesswoman.

Grace was sleeping. She was safe and loved and would be fine. So why did I feel like such a failure for leaving her?

CHAPTER TWO

Brian

February 2013

Brian whistled a song he'd heard earlier on the radio. He didn't know the words, but the tune was catchy enough. As he reached for a towel to wipe away the traces of shaving cream from his cheeks, he knocked his wedding ring off the sink ledge. It spun before dropping into the garbage pail.

He wrinkled his nose as he wiped the white cream off his face and bent down to the garbage can. It was full of mounds of Kleenex and dental floss. Gross. He nudged aside some of the garbage, hoping his ring was close to the top. No such luck. After moving the garbage aside, he found his ring lying on top of a box.

He almost dismissed the box. Almost.

Brian set his ring on the sink counter and pulled out the box. His heart skipped a beat when he realized what he was holding. With a quick glance over his shoulder, he opened it up and forgot to breathe.

A small white stick dropped into his hand and he stared down at it in amazement. He glanced up and looked across the room to call out to his wife, but stopped.

This was in the garbage. The garbage, covered with Kleenex, as if it needed to be hidden. Why would she hide this? How did he not even know she was taking it?

Brian went through the last few days in his head to see if Diane had given him any sort of hint that she might be pregnant, but there was nothing.

If he hadn't knocked his ring off the ledge, if he hadn't nudged the garbage to the side and caught sight of the box his wife hid beneath everything else, would he have found out?

His heart jumped as he stared down at the little plus sign. He knew what that meant—he'd waited for too many years to see that little pink plus sign. She was pregnant.

Pregnant.

But why hadn't she told him?

Maybe she'd just found out and was trying to process it all first. This was part of their plan. They'd given themselves ten years before they'd talk about having children, and it had been twelve. They were in their thirties now, in a good place, happy, and financially secure. Everything they'd wanted to be in place before they brought a child into the world was set.

They were going to have a baby.

Tears filled Brian's eyes as the realization hit him. An area in his heart he didn't realize had been empty was now filling up. Amazing how a little pink plus sign on a small white stick could do that.

A baby.

"Brian? Could you help?"

He quickly dropped the stick into his pocket as Diane walked toward him, turned her back, and gathered her hair in her hands. She wore a strapless black dress that sparkled as if covered with diamonds. A flash of lightning snaked through his body as he reached for the zipper, his finger brushing against her soft skin as he pulled upward.

He'd never been so turned on in his life.

With his hands, he caressed her waist before turning her toward him. A look of surprise filled her eyes moments before he slanted his mouth over hers.

She gave him a small, halfhearted push away.

"We're going to be late." A soft smile played on her lips.

"I don't care." He pulled her back in. "Let's have our own little celebration." He could think of a million ways they could celebrate tonight, and all of them were in bed between the soft satin sheets.

Diane's face lit up but she still pushed him away, untangling his hands from around her body. "We can't do that." She leaned in close and kissed him softly. "Later, okay?" she whispered.

Later.

"Promise?" He watched the way her body swayed as she made her way toward their walk-in closets.

"Promise."

He followed her, leaning against the edge of the closet door, and memorized how she looked, bathed in a soft light as she studied the rows of shoes in front of her.

"Which ones would look best?"

Brian remembered not to roll his eyes as she picked out two pair, one a soft pearl and the other black.

"You bought the soft pearl ones for this dress, didn't you?" Yes, he knew what to call them after the lecture he'd received a week earlier when she brought them home and he'd asked why she needed another pair of shoes.

Diane shrugged. "Maybe black would be better." She bit the side of her lip as she slipped one of each onto her feet.

He crossed the small room and stood beside her, pretending to deeply consider the two options.

"I think either would work, especially with you naked." He ogled his brows, loving the laughter that spilled from her lips.

"What's with you tonight? You were grumpier than all get out a half hour ago."

"That was before I found this." He was going to wait until later to confess he knew her secret but he couldn't stop himself. He pulled out the little white stick that made his dream come true and watched for the look of joy to cross his wife's face.

The last thing he expected was to have her eyes shy away from his.

He stood there as she walked away from him. Time stood still as he struggled to process what was happening.

"Diane?"

She stood at her pullout jewelry container. With careful precision, she opened it and selected the diamond earrings he'd bought her for Christmas last year. She took her time putting them on before fiddling with her hair.

He waited for her to say something. Anything. His world was crashing down around him and until she spoke, he could only wait.

"What do you want me to say? I took a pregnancy test. It came back positive. But until I go to the doctor and do an official blood test, nothing in my life has changed."

"Our life," he whispered, but loud enough that he caught her slight shrug.

"Those tests are false all the time." She turned toward him but refused to look at him, to let him read the truth in her own eyes. He always could. She might be an amazing businesswoman, able to keep her cool and keep a cold mask on her face when she needed it, but never with him. Until now.

"Why didn't you tell me? We've talked about this moment for years." His voice hitched. "You should have told me."

Diane's mouth opened then closed. Her shoulders slouched for a moment before her back straightened. He knew his wife. He knew she was placing this discussion into a box and focusing on tonight's events. He knew, even before she opened her eyes, that she was finished with a discussion that for her hadn't even started.

A slight smile gathered upon her lips as she walked toward him. She held out her hand and waited for him to grab it. He hesitated a moment, stared into her eyes, and forced her to read the multitude of emotions there: how happy he was to find out she was pregnant and how much it hurt to know she'd kept the news from him.

"I need to focus on this party for tonight. I need you to be there, with me, beside me." She squeezed his hand. "Whether I'm . . . pregnant or not . . . can we talk about that tonight? After the party? Please?" For a moment he saw the sliver of hope there. That's all he needed. To know that there was a part of her wanting to be pregnant.

Brian pulled his wife into his arms and held her close. He breathed her in deep, loving the warm vanilla scent. It brought him back to their early years, when all they focused on was each other, before they forged ahead with their goals and making five- and ten-year plans. Back then, ten years seemed like a lifetime. Back then, having children was the last thing on their minds.

Until recently. When they'd celebrated their twelfth anniversary, Brian had been the one to bring up the topic of children. He was the only man in upper management at Harper and Wainright LLC who was married and childless, a decision most people assumed was his and Diane's together, although he always caught the sympathetic glances. The worst was on the weekends, when talk of Little League or hockey games came up.

He was ready for a child's laughter to fill their house. More than ready.

"You know that times are different now, that you don't need to be afraid," he whispered.

Diane stiffened in his arms.

"I don't want to talk about this. Not now."

"You never want to talk about it. But we should. What happened to your mother—"

"Is not something I wish to discuss right now."

When she pushed herself away from him, he let her go. Just like he always did whenever he tried to bring the topic up of her mother and having a child. The mask she wore was in place, and she was right. It wasn't fair of him to bring this up, not now, when they couldn't talk about it.

"What about Charlie?"

The look Diane gave him was both murderous and disgusted. Of course she wouldn't have told her sister. Not yet, not if she wasn't ready to admit it to herself. But she eventually would. The bond between the two of them was unique, one Brian had never experienced with his own brothers.

But despite their closeness, there was one topic the two sisters never discussed. It was the only topic Brian had once promised never to bring up.

The fact their mother gave birth to their little brother, then killed him. Then herself.

CHAPTER THREE

Diane

Present–February

I miss Brian tonight. Rereading his letter Nina gave me this morning didn't help.

A couple of times a week with our morning tea she'll hand over something from him. Before he left, he'd given her a box full of letters, notes, and a few homemade word puzzles he made up for me. This was something he'd always done whenever he went away—leaving notes hidden in my drawers, beneath my pillows, in the coffee canister—always in the last place I'd expect to find them. In return, I'd leave notes in his suitcase, his computer bag, inside his shoes, and such.

I want him to come home. I need him to come home. He hasn't even seen Grace. I know it's not his fault that he couldn't be there for her birth, but how can a father not come home to see his own child? Something must have gone wrong in London for him to stay for so long and without any word. He should have returned by now.

I don't even understand why he had to go. He's only an engineer, one of many in his company. Just because he was in management didn't mean he had to be the one to do all the traveling. It was ridiculous that they would send him overseas so close to her due date. Ridiculous.

I tell Grace about Brian every night. I tell her stories about how he decorated this room for her, what kind of ice cream he'd bring home, and the quirky songs he'd sing while making dinner. I want her to recognize him when he gets home, so every night I play the recording he made for her months before she was due.

I love listening to it. I listen to the soft cadence of his voice, the enthusiasm in his love for her. I wish I could see him, touch him, and have him lie beside me at night while we sleep.

I need him.

I'll be home before you know it. That's what he said in his letter. Except he's not and I don't know why.

If I could, I would book a flight today and take Grace to see him, but the thought of getting on an airplane causes me to panic. Like now. Even thinking about it has my hands shaking and I feel like I'm about to throw up. Nina says it's all hormonal and that it'll pass if I just give it time, that there have been so many changes in my life in the recent past that it's just how my body is reacting. I'm sure Brian understands; he has to. I've sent him countless e-mails to explain, but he hasn't responded yet.

Any other woman would think her husband had left her but I'm not any other woman. I know how much my husband loves me and how hard it was for him to leave us.

I pace my bedroom, with the muted voices from the television in the loft filling what had been like white noise, until I heard the screams and cries. What channel had I left it on? I thought it was news. I thought about going to turn it off but I didn't want to leave Grace, not even for a second, even though she was fast asleep in the bassinet on my bed.

It's irrational, this fear I have, but I've come to accept it as normal. It has to be, right?

"I thought you might like some tea." Nina stood in my doorway holding a tray with a teapot and two teacups.

I glanced back toward Grace to make sure she was still asleep. I watched the way her chest rose, in and out, in and out, and the way her eyelashes fluttered. Sweet dreams, little one.

"As long as you join me," I said, motioning to my little sitting area.

This had become our daily ritual. In the evening before we both headed to bed, we would share a cup of tea and discuss how I was feeling, what the agenda for the next day would be, and if I'd taken my medication.

"Do I still need to take these?" I picked up the little bottle containing a myriad of pills and groaned. Antidepressants. I don't understand why I have to keep taking these when I feel fine, but Diane keeps insisting it would be too much of a jolt for my body to stop right now. I hate taking any sort of medication if I don't really need to.

"Just a little while longer." Nina poured tea into the teacups and then handed me a small cup of water. Her piercing eyes watched me as I swallowed the pills.

"I thought you were only to be the nanny. I don't need a nurse anymore, you know," I grumbled.

A cloud crossed Nina's face before she handed me my teacup. "You were pretty quiet at dinner today. Everything okay? Anything you want to discuss?"

My shoulders drooped as I took a sip of the hot tea and sat back in my chair. Maybe I should go and bring the bassinet over here so I could keep an eye on Grace.

"She's fine." Nina reached out and stopped me as I was about to stand up. It was weird how she seemed to know what I was going to do before I did it.

"I can't hear her breathe." So many babies still die of SIDS, and I didn't want Grace to be one of them.

"She's okay. You need to learn to relax when you're around the little doll."

I sighed as I continued to watch the bassinet. She really was a doll. Those were the first words out of my mouth when I first saw her, and nothing has changed since then. She reminded me of one of those Precious Moments dolls, with their heart-shaped lips, long eyelashes, and perfect features. That's what Grace was—perfect. My heart swelled with love for her, and all I wanted to do was hold her in my arms.

I turned my attention away from my sleeping daughter and caught the look in Nina's eyes. Pity. Compassion. Sadness. Hope.

"Don't. Don't look at me like that."

"I'm sorry, Diane. I know today was hard for you. Do you want to talk about it?"

I was entranced by the soft shade of Nina's eyes. I loved how they changed with her emotions. One moment they could be a solid brown, full and steady, and the next a lighter shade with speckles of green. What I loved most was when she held Grace, how soft they became, like dusk. It was the reason I trusted her so completely with Grace. I knew she loved her almost as much as I did.

"I didn't think going back to work would be as hard as it was."

"You live in a cocoon here, one of your own making." Nina picked up her teacup and held it in her hands.

I shrugged. My cocoon was a safe one. The only thing missing was Brian.

"Did anyone call while I was out?" I was sure I'd asked her earlier, but all I cared about the moment I walked through my front door was my daughter.

"No. No calls." She didn't even bother to hide the sigh.

That really bothered me. I was trying not to let it, but it did.

"Does he not care? This is so unlike him." No one at Harper and Wainright would return my calls either. This was where paranoia would be appropriate, except Nina had warned me that if I didn't want post-partum depression to take hold of me, then I needed to not give in to it. Like I had a choice. She seemed to think I did, or at least was trying to make me believe it. It had to be true, though; give me a clear goal and I'd focus on it one hundred percent. Right then, not dealing with depression was one such goal. I picked up my teacup and enjoyed the warmth on my cold fingers. I didn't realize I was so cold.

Nina's lips pursed before she shook her head.

"What?"

"You need to focus on yourself and put everything else aside. I know it's hard and you feel alone and"—she paused—"abandoned. But you're not. I'm here. I promised your husband I would look after you and I intend to do that for as long as you need me."

I caught a slight sheen to her eyes and didn't like it. If anything, Nina could be colder than I could. She wore a mask she rarely took off, a mask of preservation and determination. But right now, at this moment, it was gone.

"I know you will." I leaned forward and covered her hand with my own. No other words needed to be said.

Nina nodded, lifted her chin, and swallowed. I could see the struggle to compose herself. I wonder what it was that caused that momentary break in her facade?

We both sipped at our tea.

"What show was on the television earlier?"

"What do you mean?" Nina cocked her head.

"Seemed to be a lot of screaming and then crying. Were you watching a movie?"

Nina shook her head before refilling both our cups. "Why don't you tell me about your day."

I glanced back toward Grace and relaxed in my chair. Where would I even begin? The crazy conversation with Walter about my mental state and if I was ready to resume working full time, or the way Amanda would talk to me, as if she knew more about what was going on than I did? The lunch meeting where I had to put out too many fires of Walter's making? Or the times I locked myself in the bathroom and cried because I missed Grace and Brian so much?

"It was exhausting. This whole day has been . . . tough. I wasn't prepared."

"I'm sorry, Diane. I wish I could be of more help. You don't have to carry such a heavy load. You do understand that, right?"

I nodded.

"How about going for a walk in the park in the morning then, before you begin your day?"

I almost choked on my tea. A walk? Going into work was one thing, but taking Grace out in public, where she could pick up germs, get bitten by annoying insects, and be exposed to toxins in the air? No, I wasn't ready for that. I shook my head and stared down at my lap. My fingernails looked horrid. When was the last time I'd had a manicure? And my rings. I had to remember to put my wedding rings back on tomorrow.

"Just a short one; it'll be good for you."

"I'm not sure Grace is ready yet. I should wait a little bit longer before I take her out in public, don't you think?"

Nina stood up and gathered the cups and teapot back onto the tray. I noticed she hardly gave Grace a glance.

"I think it would do you a world of good." She held the tray in her hands and stared me straight in the eye, daring me to say no.

I bit my lip. I wanted to, I really did. Why was it that I could be in control at work and yet be so . . . insecure here at home?

"Okay." I gave in. I had to pick my battles and this wasn't worth the fight. But it would be on my terms.

"Just a small one. First thing in the morning, so I have time to shower and get ready for work. I could do with the exercise anyway. It might help with the headaches I've been having lately."

I could tell this grabbed her attention. Her back had already been turned, but she stopped.

"Why haven't you mentioned them?" Her voice was very controlled and soft.

"They're just headaches." I shrugged. I headed back toward the bed where Grace lay. She looked like an angel sleeping there in her bassinet.

Brian had picked it out, surprising me at home one day with an extra-large gift-wrapped box. It was quite heavy and he wouldn't let me lift it; instead, he placed it on the bed and watched as I opened it. Inside was a beautiful basket with tightly woven strands covered in the softest cream cashmere blanket I've ever touched. It was perfect. We'd already picked out a crib, rocking chair, and changing table, but I couldn't decide on this last item.

"Starting tomorrow we're going to keep a log of these headaches, their severity, how long they last, and so on. I can't help you unless I know what you are going through."

Nina's voice startled me. I'd been so focused on Grace, I'd forgotten she was still in the room. I didn't bother to respond, since it was just a simple headache, one I got most mornings. They normally disappeared after a few hours. Nothing to get all worked up about.

CHAPTER FOUR

Brian

February 2013

Brian surveyed the reception area as he stood at the bar waiting for his order. Diane was in her element; there was brilliance about her as she swept across the room, meeting staff and their family members, having her picture taken by the press, and keeping close to Walter Dube, CEO of HK Solutions and Diane's mentor and father figure.

A woman passed by him, her bare arm lingering a little too long and close. He plastered a smile on his face as she batted her false eyelashes. With all of the low-cut dresses around, he made sure to keep his eyes focused upward.

Diane's laughter floated across the room. Brian glanced over to the bartender and found two glasses in front of him. He dipped his head in thanks and excused himself from the woman attempting to drape herself across him.

Brian made his way across the room to his wife. A waiter was at her side, holding a tray of champagne flutes. Without glancing at either the waiter or the tray, Diane reached out, curling her fingers around a glass. She continued to stand there, listening to Walter speak to a man at his side. She wore her mask, the one that mesmerized her clients while demoralizing anyone who got in her way when it came to business. It always amazed him that no one saw through it to her soft interior.

The sight of the flute in her hand made Brian pause, but only for a moment. Diane rarely drank at functions; in fact, she made it a habit never to finish a full glass. She would always hold one in her hand, but it was more part of her outfit, rather than a necessity. Brian, on the other hand, always imbibed. Only enough to get him through the night, but never more than what he could handle.

He hated these kinds of parties. He was a nerd at heart, more comfortable in front of a computer staring at code than attempting to make inane conversation with people he didn't know.

Once at Diane's side, he took the flute from her hand, placed it on a passing waiter's tray, and handed her a glass of Perrier with a slice of lime. She stepped to the side, making room for him to stand by her, and gave him a sweet smile.

Brian took a sip of his merlot and waited for the perfect moment to nudge his wife to the side to speak to her. He leaned forward and whispered into her ear, "Only a few more minutes until dinner is served. They're about to open the doors."

"Thank God. My feet are killing me." She took a sip of her drink and grimaced. "That's not champagne."

Brian frowned. "Of course not. You can't be drinking now."

Diane's eyes widened at his words while he took a step back. Did she not think of that beforehand?

"Have you?" His voice rose and he caught the quick turn of Walter's attention toward them.

She shook her head, bewilderment still alive in her eyes. "Of course not," she whispered.

From the corner of his eye, Brian caught the look between Walter and his wife. Brian's lips thinned but he remained silent.

There was something about Walter that always put him on edge. To be honest, he knew it was due to his own insecurity. Walter held a piece of Diane's heart that Brian could never touch; he'd been there for her in the very beginning, when Diane and Charlie were left alone without a father figure. Walter had given Diane her first job and made sure Charlie made it through nursing school when their aunt had run out of money.

Brian had once joked that if push came to shove, Diane would choose Walter over him. She'd hesitated a moment too long before denying his claim, but that moment was all it took, and he never pushed. Besides, his job as senior VP at Harper and Wainright LLC, an international engineering firm, had him traveling close to thirty weeks in a year. Because they respected each other's choices, both personal and professional, their marriage had lasted for over twelve years.

Audible sighs of excitement filled the air as people entered the reception area. Diane's fingers squeezed his arm. He glanced down and winked at her. The elegance of the room might be lost on him but he knew she'd worked hard on the decor.

This was, after all, a night to celebrate her.

"I should have gone with the white and black look," Diane muttered.

Brian glanced at the table and shrugged. "Why?" He thought it looked just fine. Well, except for the fact the tables were too cluttered with tall glasses full of light blue and white marbles with a candle sitting on top. Why did women insist on filling tables up until there was no room left for anything else? He looked at the glass in his hand and then at the two glasses situated to the right of each dinner plate. What did he need those glasses for? Thank God he wasn't the one doing the dishes.

"They look fine, even if it's not black. Stop stressing about it." He followed his wife to their table, the front table off to the right, and pulled out her chair. Diane held on to it but never sat down. Instead, she viewed the room, taking in every table and who was sitting where. He could read her mind; somewhere in the room, someone was in the wrong spot.

"How many hours did you spend putting together the seating arrangement?"

"About as long as it took you to set up that new office in Hungary."

Brian groaned. He still had nightmares about that trip.

"Couldn't Amanda have handled all this for you?"

Diane frowned as she handed her empty glass of water to a waiter passing by.

"Not with all the media present. I think Walter has something big he plans on announcing tonight."

"You think? Shouldn't you know?"

Diane shrugged her shoulders. "You would think so, but whatever it is, he's keeping it a secret." She squeezed his hand before stepping away to talk to a couple a few tables over.

Brian sat and pulled out his phone. He was in for a long night, so he might as well respond to the pile of e-mails sure to be filling his inbox. No one ever said being the head of a department was a nine-to-five job.

"Where's that gorgeous wife of yours?" Walter's boisterous voice bellowed across the room.

He pocketed his phone and twisted in his chair to catch Walter heading toward him. Brian had first met Walter almost immediately after he had started to date Diane. Back then, Walter had been a trim man who ran every day and rarely drank. A few wives later, that had all changed. Tonight, Walter looked like a stuffed penguin in his black suit. Rolls of grotesque skin rolled over the man's collar as he waddled across the room. At least he knew enough not to pull a Donald Trump and shaved off what few strands of hair he had left.

Brian pushed out his chair and stood. He might not necessarily like the man and he might think he took advantage of Diane too often, but he had to play nice.

"Walter." Brian held out his hand and forced himself not to grimace at Walter's sweaty grip.

"Where is that girl of ours? I've hardly said a word to her tonight."

Brian kept a tight smile on his face. "My wife"—heavy emphasis on the *my*—"is around somewhere." He thrust his hands in his jacket pockets and turned on his heel slightly so as to look over the crowd, when in truth, he didn't want to encourage any small talk.

"Tonight's a big night for her." The force of Walter's hand slapping Brian's back pushed him forward. "Her whole world is about to change and I couldn't be happier. She deserves it."

Brian glanced back at Walter. How did he know? Surely, Diane wouldn't have told Walter their news yet, when they hadn't even had the chance to talk themselves. She wouldn't do that.

"What are you boys talking about?" Diane laced her arm through Brian's as she came up behind him.

Brian leaned over and placed a small kiss upon her cheek. "About how awesome you are, honey."

Diane beamed up at him. There was a light in her eyes that mesmerized him. His heart raced at the thought of why she was so happy. Those earlier misgivings must have passed. The reality of the life growing inside her must have hit her.

The noise in the large room stilled as Diane clinked her butter knife against the water glasses. Walter made his way up the stairs, stood at the podium, and tugged his suit coat down.

She sat beside Brian, her fingers knotted together. He knew she was nervous. This was a big night for her. A night she'd worked hard at for a long time. She deserved every single moment.

He couldn't help but wonder how all of this would change once their baby was born.

Brian reached out and threaded his fingers through hers. He rubbed the pad of his thumb against her smooth skin and couldn't believe how cold she was.

"I want to thank y'all for coming tonight. This is a night of celebrations. A lot of great things have happened at HK Solutions, but let me tell you"—Walter paused for what Brian knew to be dramatic effect—"none of it could have happened without each and every one of you tonight. Give yourselves a round of applause; you deserve it!" Feedback screeched through the sound system as Walter clapped his hands right in front of the microphone. Brian winced and shot the sound guys over in the corner a look. The two of them were shaking their heads while fiddling with their soundboards.

Diane wrenched her hand from Brian's and clapped, a strained look filling her face as she kept her attention focused forward.

While Walter's voice droned on, Brian studied his wife. Something was wrong; he could tell. There was no sparkle in her eye, no excitement over tonight's events, especially since this part was about her. Every bone in her body was rigid with tension, every movement precise.

He moved his chair closer and laid his arm on the back of her chair. She jumped the moment he placed his hand on her shoulder.

"Relax. Walter's not going to do anything stupid." He winked. "Okay, so maybe he doesn't have the greatest of track records, but he's been good so far, right?"

Years ago, Walter announced a crazy new idea in the middle of a speech and told the crowd that it would reinvent the digital age for the blind in a way that would astound the world. Diane had to burn the midnight oil just to figure out what Walter had wanted, and it took a while, but his scheme of being the first software company in San Francisco to offer speech-to-text software had come to pass.

"There's always a first time, right?" A small smile played on her lips.

"Right." Brian nodded, satisfied to see that smile.

Walter continued, sharing stats about how well the company did in the last year compared to the year before and about their growth and expansion in the area of distribution. He caught Diane's lips moving and knew she'd written his speech for him.

"It's time," Diane mumbled.

"Finally," Brian groaned. Diane elbowed him while Neil snickered away beside him. Brian flashed the guy a smile.

"Before we end our night, there are a few people in this room I'd like to recognize for their dedication, for their motivation, and for keeping me on my toes."

A smattering of laughter filled the room while Walter puffed out his chest. Brian was tempted to count the seconds before a button popped.

"First off, Neil, why don't you come on up here?"

Brian couldn't keep the smile off his face as a startled Neil rose from his seat and buttoned up his jacket. "What's going on?" Neil whispered to Diane.

"Go on up." Diane smiled and started to clap her hands, which forced the rest of the table and then the room to join along with her.

Brian felt sorry for Neil. The poor guy's cheeks flamed, and he almost tripped going up the stairs. Walter was there to lend him a hand.

"Neil here is one of those guys who like to keep me on my toes. He's always coming to me with new ideas, wanting to buy new equipment that will increase our productivity, and forcing me to slow down on my innovative dreaming. Apparently, what I want isn't always available, and I need guys like Neil to keep me on the straight and narrow."

Brian didn't think Neil's face could turn another shade of red, but it did right there. "Neil"—the audible slap from Walter to Neil's back echoed through the microphone—"you've shown nothing but dedication to this company. You've proved to me over and over that you are a man I need to keep by my side. So it's with that in mind that I've decided to make you head of our technical department! Congratulations!" Walter stepped back and thundered his hands together, the smile spread wide across his face. Brian stood up beside Diane to show their support.

Neil stood there with a goofy grin on his face. "Ah, wow, ah . . . thank you."

"Now, just don't be letting it go to your head. Remember, I'm still in charge of this company, and we can't be installing all those newfangled pieces of equipment you want to requisition." He winked at Neil.

"Let's talk on Monday." Neil shrugged. Walter struggled with his words while Diane almost choked on her sip of water.

Thunderous applause filled the room while Neil stepped off the podium. Brian shook the stunned man's hand.

"You deserve it, man."

Neil pushed his glasses up. "It's just a glorified title."

Brian smiled sympathetically and moved off to the side for Diane. She hugged Neil, placing her lips close to his ear. Brian couldn't make out what she said, but no doubt it was a threat coated with honey, if Neil's slumped shoulders gave any indication. He knew how much Diane fought to keep Neil in Walter's good graces. If Walter had his way, Neil would have been sent packing over a year ago, after Walter crashed their network and Neil yelled at him for his carelessness.

"Diane, why don't you come on up here," Walter called out.

Brian grabbed his wife's hand. A fragile look crossed her face.

"I love you," he whispered. There was a slight tremble to her lips before she blew him a kiss and headed toward the stage.

What was going on? She'd been so excited about tonight. This was the night she'd worked so hard for—why did she seem hesitant? Whatever Walter had in store, he just hoped it wouldn't put too much pressure on Diane.

Once again applause filled the room as Diane took the stage. Brian puffed out his chest, proud to call the hot woman who commanded the room his wife.

"This woman here is a cornerstone to our company. I may have known her since she was a teenager with a mind of her own, but I knew from that moment that she was someone special. Through thick and thin she's been by my side as HK Solutions grew to become the company I knew it could be. I couldn't trust anyone more than I trust this woman. And, folks, without Diane, we wouldn't be where we are today. She's not only the perfect business partner but also a dear friend and part of my family. She's the daughter I never had but always wanted, and I'm very glad to have her by my side as we forge new grounds in the exciting world of creating software for the visually impaired together."

"Aww. How sweet," Neil muttered.

"I am very proud to announce that"—there was a slight pause— "Diane Wright is no longer the vice president of HK Solutions, but is now the new CEO while I take on the role of chief operating officer!"

A round of enthusiastic applause followed his announcement.

"Did he just say what I thought he said?" Neil asked.

Brian sat there in stunned silence before he jumped from his seat and clapped furiously. This was it! Everything Diane had worked so hard for. They'd expected Walter to announce one year of training where Diane would work side by side with Walter before she took on the role of president. But this was more. More than expected. More than anticipated. He couldn't be prouder of her in this moment.

No wonder Walter had insisted on the media being present.

From the brightness of her smile and the way she reached for the edge of the podium for support, Brian could tell she hadn't expected this either. He mouthed his love to her and saw it reflected back in her eyes before she turned back to Walter and placed her arms around him and hugged him close.

Tonight, with this announcement, all of Diane's dreams had come true.

So where did having a baby fit into the picture for them?

CHAPTER FIVE

Diane

Present–March

Mozart played in the background as I sat in the rocker we'd bought for Grace's room. I stared down at her in my arms. It seemed like that was all I ever did. I could stare at her for hours on end, and in reality, I did.

It was hard not to. She was the most perfect baby I had ever seen in my life.

I grabbed my phone and snapped a picture to send to Brian. I must have sent him more than a hundred photos since we'd come home from the hospital. I didn't want him to miss out on a single moment.

"Your daddy will fall in love with you the moment he holds you in his arms. I know it."

I held her in the crook of my arm and waited for her to smile. Her smile reminded me of Brian, which made me miss him all the more. This morning I'd worked on a word search puzzle he'd made for me, a love puzzle. It made me smile to circle words like *sweetheart* and *ice cream sundae*, knowing that he picked each word with a specific memory in mind.

"Diane?" Nina poked her head into the room. "Why don't you come out and join me for a cup of tea?"

"I'd love that." I pushed myself up from the chair, careful not to bump Grace while I did so.

Little by little things were getting easier. Being a mother wasn't as easy as I thought, even with a nanny in the house. When I was home, I wanted to be the one to take care of my daughter; at least, that was what I thought I had wanted. But more and more, I'd come to depend on Nina to help me, even with the little things like heating up the bottles or figuring out why Grace cried when there seemed to be no reason.

"Why don't you put her down for a nap?" Nina came in and placed a fresh blanket down in the bassinet I had set in the crib.

I bit my lip. I really didn't want to put her down. I loved holding her.

"The little angel will be fine. The monitor is turned on so you'll hear every sound."

I still hesitated.

"We should set up a playpen or something for her to sleep in downstairs." I preferred to keep her close.

"Trust me?" A few wisps had escaped from Nina's ponytail and dangled in front of her face. She reached for Grace and I relinquished her without thought. The moment she left my arms I winced. I shouldn't have done that. I could have put her down. I needed to learn to do things on my own more and more. Nina wasn't going to be here forever.

"I do." I sighed. "Will I ever get the hang of this?"

Nina placed Grace down in her bed. I stood beside my baby and straightened her dress. I loved this outfit. It was one I'd picked out online just a few weeks ago. A soft cream dress with a dark pink ribbon on the hem, sleeves and neckline. The dress was quite long, down to her toes, so I didn't have any leggings on her. I found them quite tiresome to get off when I needed to change her. Instead, I found some knitted booties in the dresser drawer, a gift from Walter while I'd been on bed rest. That hadn't been the only thing he'd sent either. Almost daily, either a package would arrive or he'd come over in the evening and bring me something, a blanket, an outfit, or something special for me. That stopped, though, once I brought Grace home. He'd come over once with a gift-wrapped box and left it at the front door when no one had answered, and inside was a doll for Grace. Since then though, he'd kept his distance, which bothered me more than I wanted to admit.

"Sweet dreams, my little princess." I bent down to kiss her.

How could it be possible to love a child as much as I loved her?

I closed the door to her room and followed Nina down the stairs. A fresh wind blew through the open windows at the bottom of the staircase.

A tray was on the kitchen counter with tea and a plate of cut fruit along with baked scones.

"I thought we could maybe sit outside today?"

The scones looked delicious. I loved to cook but could never bake, and once Nina realized how much I loved homemade baked goods, she would spoil me once a week with muffins, cakes, or scones. My favorites were her croissants and vanilla scones, which she brought today. She cut a few slices of butter and placed them on a small plate and my mouth watered. I made my way to the back door but Nina stopped me.

"I thought maybe we could sit on the front porch instead?"

I froze. My throat dried up so I couldn't swallow and a sudden chill swept over me, forcing the hairs on my arms to stand on end.

"I'd rather sit in the back." My voice warbled a bit.

"Have you noticed the flower beds in the front? The tulips are just starting to come up and you can see the lilacs starting to bloom. My mother used to have lilac bushes in our front yard growing up; I'd forgotten how much I loved the scent." Nina babbled as she took my hand and turned me away from the back door. "Could you carry the tray? Be careful, though; the pot is full. I'll grab the monitor and a blanket in case you get chilled with the wind." She handed me the tray. Whether I wanted to or not, I was going out to the front.

It's not that I didn't like sitting on the front patio, it was just that I couldn't.

Once upon a time, I used to go running early in the mornings. I'd get up, lace my sneakers, pull my hair back in a ponytail, and head outdoors. It didn't matter whether the sun shone or storm clouds were rolling in. I used to go running through the paths that circled the downtown core, always stopping at a local coffee shop and chatting with the early morning servers while I sipped at my chai latte.

When we moved to this new house, one thing I loved was that we were blocks away from a city park where I could run. I looked forward to getting back into the groove after Grace was born. I even bought one of those joggers so I could take her with me, but since her birth, I'd been hesitant to head outside. The most I'd done was to sit out on our backyard patio and soak up the sun for a few brief minutes while I made sure Grace stayed in the shade and sheltered from any bugs.

I could head to work, no problem. I could run errands during work hours and on my way home, but the moment anything else was required of me I panicked.

Like right now.

"You can do this, Diane." Nina led the way while I trailed behind.

I'd mentally prepared myself for the sleepless nights, for my ineptness when it came to having a newborn. But nothing prepared me for the emotional aspect. I was strong in so many ways, but when it came to facing the public with Grace, I couldn't do it.

It was as if there was a deep fear that something would go wrong and I wouldn't know how to handle the situation. What if she fell? What if she cried and I couldn't get her to stop? What if she got sick— or worse, died—and there was nothing I could do?

It was safer to stay home, where I knew I wasn't alone.

"Remember, Grace is safe in her bed. It's just you and me having a cup of tea." Nina held the door open for me, an encouraging smile filling her face.

Right. It was just me. Grace was safe. This was no different than if I were heading to work or having a coffee on the patio of some cafe. I could do this.

Except I couldn't. My feet were rooted and refused to budge and my heart was about to rip out of my chest. I could feel it pushing against my ribs with each beat. I stared at Nina, at the door, and then at the tray in my hands, and felt like I was Alice in Wonderland looking down at everything that suddenly shrank in size. The floor beneath me caved in and I would have fallen through, I know I would have, if Nina hadn't reached out and steadied me.

The teacups rattled and hot liquid splashed onto the tray, droplets landing on my fingers as I gripped the handle.

"Deep breath, Diane. A deep breath."

Nina breathed in and I followed her example. We breathed out together. She took a few steps backward and pushed open the screen door. I took one step forward, then another. I tried to ignore the pressure in my chest and the fact that my eyes were filling with tears. I tried to ignore everything except for the woman who waited for me to step outside.

My hands shook but I took another step. I had tunnel vision. I focused on Nina and her smile.

The moment I did it, the moment I crossed the threshold and stepped onto the porch, the weight that pressed so hard against my chest lifted. It was strange. I drank in the sunshine, the fresh air, and the feel of life around me. Nina took hold of the tray and set it down on the wicker table.

"Did something happen to the furniture? I thought it was white?" We'd picked up a set at a local garage sale when we'd first moved in. Brian had been determined to blend in; he didn't want us to have the "condo" look about us, even though I thought whatever look we had would fit in. We used to tour the garage sales when we were first married but now we never took the time. The odd Saturday we had off we enjoyed lounging in bed and eating fresh croissants with our coffee while checking the news. But there had been a community garage sale and so Brian felt it would be a good way to get to know our neighbors. And get to know them we did.

Bob and Jenny lived down the street with four kids. Chad and Natasha lived two doors down with a house full of dogs. Sherri and Darryl lived a block over with their hockey team's worth of kids. Every couple we met had children. We seemed to be the only childless couple around, unless you counted Doug and Leona, who lived next door. They were a bit older and no doubt would have grandchildren running around their yard sooner or later.

We had meals brought over to us to welcome us to the neighborhood after that garage sale, and had more comments than I could count on the wicker set we'd bought from some house across the park. It almost felt like *Desperate Housewives*. I kept waiting for Bree Van de Kamp to show up with a basket of fresh-baked muffins.

"See, isn't this nice?" Nina ignored my comment and sat down before she poured the tea. I could tell the brew was a bit strong, but that was my fault.

I sank down in my chair and let out a long sigh. This was nice. It was a beautiful day.

Nina set the baby monitor down on the table between us and turned up the volume. I smiled my thanks and leaned back, soaking in the fresh outdoors and willing myself to relax.

One step at a time. That was all it took. One step until I was back to being the woman I used to be. I had no idea I'd change in such a drastic way once I had Grace. No one had prepared me for the emotional influx and insecurities.

"Have you heard from Brian at all?" It seemed like forever since I last spoke with my husband. I knew he was busy; he was always busy when overseas, and the time difference didn't help that much. He once told me that his goal when away was to make it home ahead of schedule, so I hated to bother him.

"The phone has been very quiet lately." Nina sipped at her tea, her focus out on the lawn.

"Why hasn't he called? It's not like him at all. He should be home any day, but I don't even know his itinerary." I bit my lip. "I don't even know if he's seen any of the pictures I've sent him of Grace."

Nina placed her cup down on the tray. I noticed the way she turned slowly toward me. I wondered whether she hurt her back somehow.

"You have? Taken pictures?"

I nodded.

"I love taking photos of her. I should work on her baby album as well. I saw it this morning in her room. I'd almost forgotten about it."

"So did I." Nina's voice was quiet. She glanced my way, a quick, furtive look.

"Maybe"—I smiled at Nina—"that will be my afternoon project. We could sit outside in the back and go through it together. The first few days after Grace's birth are a bit fuzzy, so I'll need you to help fill in the blanks."

"I thought maybe we could go for a walk today. Get some exercise with this fresh air. Remember, you wanted to start running again?"

Nina had been quick to ignore my idea, I noticed.

"I'm not quite ready for a walk. I'd rather just relax today with Grace and work on the baby album."

Nina sighed. "I really do wish you'd consider a walk. We can work on the album afterward."

The thought of taking Grace out in public, on a walk where everyone would gawk and want to touch her, hold her, breathe their germs on her . . . no. It was too soon.

One step at a time. But they had to be steps I was willing to take. Not ones Nina forced on me.

I knew she was worried about me. About my mental state. I overheard her last night on the phone. She was concerned that I was withdrawing and using Grace as an excuse. Except that wasn't true.

Was I withdrawing? Yes. Of course I was. I could feel it. It was as if my brain couldn't handle the person I used to be. That Diane was a workaholic and this Diane was a mother. I wasn't sure how to merge the two identities. But was it a cause for alarm? Hardly. This had to be normal for most working mothers. The idea of having only a short period of time to adjust to having a child was ridiculous.

And I wasn't ready to make the change. Plain and simple.

"Oh, look, you have guests." Nina's voice perked up as she stood.

Chad and Natasha, our neighbors two doors down, were headed our way. Their arms were linked while Natasha carried a basket. I liked them. Both Brian and I thought they were very real and personable. I even thought that Natasha and I might develop a friendship of sorts.

My hands shook as I sat there.

"Diane, come and say hi," Nina said over her shoulder. Her voice was soft, so as not to carry.

I gave a small shake of my head and swallowed past the lump in my throat. I didn't want to say hi to anyone. I didn't want to converse, chat, or make any kind of small talk. I didn't want to have to explain anything to anyone about anything and I knew that is what I'd have to do. *Where is Brian? How is Grace? We haven't seen you out lately.*

This was my life and no one else's. I didn't need busybodies in my way.

I jumped up from my chair and grabbed the baby monitor.

"I hear Grace. Say hi for me." I rushed past her, and the screen door slammed behind me.

I sank down on the bottom step of the stairs leading to the second floor, hidden away from prying eyes but close enough to listen to the conversation.

"We just . . . wanted to drop these off and see if there was anything we could do for Diane," Natasha said.

"Thank you. I'm sure she'll love this," Nina spoke up. She knew I remained close by.

"This has to be such a difficult time for her." Natasha's sweet voice held a note of sympathy that hit me hard.

Why would she feel sorry for me? We barely knew each other. And why was this such a difficult time for me? Because Brian was away?

"Thank you. I know she'll love them." Nina repeated her earlier statement.

There was a moment of silence. I straightened up to look out the window and caught Chad's gaze. There was a look in his eye—regret? Pity? I wasn't sure.

"Let her know we are here if she ever needs us. With Brian's . . ." Chad's voice faltered when Nina coughed. "Right, well, um, well, we're here. I'll keep the grass trimmed, and all that . . . stuff."

"And I'd be more than happy to give you a break if you wanted one," Natasha added. "You know, to sit with Diane and have a cup of coffee or something. I'd been meaning to bake a cake lately. What's her favorite kind? Do you think she'd like that?"

I sank back down on the step and hugged my knees. From the way they talked, I sounded like a charity case.

Was I?

———

Shadows grew along the floor as I wandered aimlessly through the silent house with Grace in my arms.

I wasn't one for silence. There was something about it that unnerved me.

If Brian were there, he'd have teased me that I don't like to be alone with my own thoughts. He'd be partially right.

I preferred to be surrounded by sound, whether it was music, the television, or the hum of the dishwasher. It really didn't matter, as long as I wasn't left alone in silence.

When I was growing up, our house was always quiet. Too quiet. My dad would sit in front of the muted television while he drank endless bottles of beer. I never understood how he could make it into work the next day until I realized he was a functioning alcoholic. It took me years to figure that out. I never knew, in that silence, what he would do if I were to turn my music up or ask him a question.

I knew Nina didn't like it, but I needed noise. I had a feeling she went throughout the day with the radio on low, whereas I always ended turning the volume up when I was home. I even left the television on upstairs in the loft.

I knew Grace liked the noise. She seemed to sleep better, and smiled when I sang to her.

I was restless, but not sure what it was I wanted or even needed to do.

"We're housebound with nothing to do." I kissed the top of Grace's head as I made my way into my office.

It felt like forever since I'd last been in here. I'd told Nina to make use of it if she needed it. When I was on bed rest, I just stayed in my room. And since Grace . . . well, until recently, work had been the last thing on my mind.

I will admit, though, as hard as it was, going into the office had felt good.

Instead of going back full-time, I took Nina's suggestion and started with two days a week. I'll work my way up little by little, until I was more comfortable with leaving Grace for that long.

I sat down in my big office chair and turned it so the sun was on my face.

It beckoned me, calling to me to go back outside. I enjoyed it this morning. I almost felt normal, like all was right in my world.

Sad how one small event could make me feel that way.

I held Grace in front of me and had her stand on my legs. She was wobbly, but she seemed to enjoy bobbing up and down.

From the corner of my eye I noticed a vehicle turn into my driveway, one I didn't recognize. But the moment the car door opened, I knew who it was.

I pushed myself up from the chair with excitement and rushed to the front door with Grace in my arms.

My baby sister was here.

"Charlie!" I stood a few feet away from the screen door and waited for her to come in. Except she just stood there.

"Come in, come in." I danced on the spot as I waited for her to open the door.

It felt like years since I'd last seen her. But in reality, it had been only months. I couldn't believe how much I missed her.

"Dee, you look . . . Oh my God, I've missed you." She hesitated a few moments once inside before she dropped her bags on the floor and hugged me.

I wrapped my free arm around her as I snuggled Grace in tight to my body.

Both of us had tears in our eyes as we looked at each other.

"It's been too long," we both said in unison before we laughed.

We used to do that all the time, share the same thought and speak it at the same time.

"What are you doing here? Where's Marcus?" I was so happy to see her. I felt like a lightbulb had been turned on inside of me and I could hardly contain my excitement. "I thought you would still be in the Congo or some other godforsaken place."

Charlie worked for Doctors Without Borders as a pediatric nurse along with her fiancé, Dr. Marcus Hilroy.

"I took some vacation time to spend with my big sis." Charlie planted a kiss on my cheek before she glanced at Grace.

Finally! I couldn't wait to introduce them.

"Charlie, meet your niece, Grace." I held Grace out and waited for Charlie to take her. It was very rare for me to let anyone other than Nina hold Grace, but this was different.

Charlie hesitated before she gathered Grace in her arms. For a moment it looked like she didn't know what to do with a baby. She jostled Grace around a bit before she got her settled in the crook of her arm.

"Isn't she beautiful? She reminds me of one of those Precious Moments figurines Mags used to make us dust every Saturday morning before we were allowed to go out to play."

Our Aunt Maggie raised us after our mother's death. She was amazing, and I wished she could have met Grace. She would have loved her. Unfortunately, Mags had passed away from breast cancer three years earlier.

A crooked smile formed on Charlie's face.

"Remember how mad she got when we broke a few pieces?" Mirth danced in her eyes at the memory.

I laughed. I'd forgotten all about that. Aunt Mags rarely disciplined us, but that day we'd been caught fooling around with her figurines when we were supposed to be dusting the shelves. Charlie had dropped one, but I covered up for it and said it was my fault. She knew we'd been lying and she sent us to our room with only toast and milk for supper.

"She was more upset with us for lying than for her doll being broken." I gazed at Grace in Charlie's arms. "She looks just like one of those dolls." I reached for Grace, wanting her back in my arms.

"That she does." Charlie rubbed the back of her neck while she looked around.

I eyed the bags by the front door. "How long can you stay?"

"As long as you need me."

I didn't know how to respond to that. Charlie rarely stayed in one place long when she was in between missions with Doctors Without Borders. She loved to see the world and experience new things. In her late twenties and newly engaged, she rarely traveled anywhere without Marcus now, and they preferred to keep their downtime as light and carefree as they could, which never surprised me. Charlie was a ray of sunshine in an otherwise dark world. She always had been. I worked hard to make sure she was never touched by the heartache in our lives.

I led the way down the hallway and trusted she'd follow along.

"Coffee?" I called over my shoulder.

"Dear Lord, yes, please! I came straight from the airport and haven't had a good cup of coffee since my layover at Heathrow."

I set Grace down in the playpen I'd set up earlier when Nina had first left and grabbed the carafe of coffee I'd made earlier.

"So what's with the sudden visit? I thought you wouldn't be back till Christmas this time?" I poured two cups before she answered, filled them both with cream, and set them on the table. I then grabbed two scones from a container and placed them by a small container with butter and jam.

"They let you near a stove?" Charlie eyed the scones.

"What? Ha ha, very funny." I loved to cook, but Brian was the baker in the family. No matter how many times I tried, the only things I could bake came out of a box and all I had to do was mix and pour.

"Store bought?" Charlie sighed as she cut her scone and started to slather jam on it.

"No, my nanny's quite the baker."

Charlie's hand stilled. "A na . . . nanny?" She stumbled over the word.

She must be tired. I explained how Nina came to stay with us and tried to dismiss the concern in her eyes.

"I wish Brian were here. He'd love to see you. You should have called him when you landed in London. I'm sure he would have come to see you. He was quite jealous about this latest trip of yours, you know. It's always been a dream of his to go to Africa."

"About that." She stirred her coffee and wouldn't look me in the eyes. "How are you doing?"

"Fine." I shrugged. "It's hard not having him here, raising Grace alone. But . . ." Charlie put her hand on mine and I glanced over at my little girl. Yes, it was hard being a single parent, but I wouldn't trade having Grace for the world. Besides, it wouldn't be for long. Brian would come home soon. Putting my hand over Charlie's, I asked, "Does Walter know you're back? You know he'd love to see you."

"I called him when I landed." She stared down at the floor.

I tried not to let that bother me, but it did.

"I should invite him over for dinner. It's been a while since he's been by."

Charlie winced. "I think he mentioned plans tonight. I told him I'd drop by for coffee one day soon."

"Or"—I smiled—"he could come here. You know, I don't think he's ever met Grace. Oh wait . . . he stopped by once and left a gift. A doll, actually."

"A doll." Charlie turned her head slightly away from me and glanced over toward Grace.

"It's so cute. It almost looks exactly like Grace too. You'll have to see it." I kept the doll in Grace's crib. I couldn't wait till she was older and played with it.

I picked up my coffee cup and smiled. "Do you remember how Mags used to love holding a hot cup of water between her hands? She swore it was the fastest way to warm up a body."

"I do." Charlie nodded. "What's with the avoidance?" She reached for my hand. "How are you doing?"

"I'm fine. Is that what you want to hear? I'm fine." I knew what she was hinting at, but I wasn't about to go there. All discussions of our mother were strictly prohibited.

"Diane." Charlie sighed. "Don't shut me out, okay? I'm worried about you. For you. I came back as soon as I could. This isn't a time for you to be alone."

"Have you looked at yourself lately? Maybe I should be the one worrying." I tried to keep my mouth shut, but she honestly looked horrible. Dark circles beneath her eyes, hair pulled back in a tattered ponytail, a shirt that looked like it needed to be thrown out. "When was the last time you had a shower?"

"I was in the Congo, Diane. Not a spa. And you know I never sleep well on the plane."

"Then go upstairs, take a shower, and have a nap. I need to put Grace to bed anyway. You'll need to sleep in the loft, though; is that okay? Nina sleeps in the spare bedroom." I made a mental note to talk to Nina about setting up a bed in Grace's room for Charlie. It wasn't like we used her room a lot anyway.

"Nina?"

"Our nanny. You'll like her; she's also a nurse."

Charlie gripped the edge of the table to stand but hesitated.

"Listen, Diane. There's another reason why I'm here." She glanced over at the playpen where Grace slept with a sad smile on her face.

I knew right away what she was going to say.

"Charlie! I'm so happy for you!" I rushed over and enveloped her in a large hug and was shocked when she pushed me away.

"What?" Her brows knitted in confusion.

"Oh . . . I . . . I just thought." I stumbled over my words, embarrassed that I'd read her so wrong.

Charlie twirled the end of her long ponytail in her fingers.

"You thought I was pregnant?" She blew a puff of air out of her mouth and stared at the ceiling. "No, but that's what I wanted us to talk about."

Grace started to whine and I knew it was only a matter of time before she'd start to cry. That was one sound I hated more than anything else in the world, her cries. It broke my heart each time.

"Listen, go have a shower." I squeezed her hand. "We can talk after, okay?"

"I won't be long, okay? I'll be back before you know it." There was a look in Charlie's eyes that I didn't like to see. Worry.

"Of course you won't be long. You're only going upstairs." I picked up Grace from where she lay and the moment she saw my face her eyes lit up. I held her close, smoothed her hair, and straightened the cute little outfit I dressed her in today, and almost didn't notice Charlie's retreat from the kitchen. I caught a brief glimpse of her as she hoisted her bags over her shoulder. I was about to call out to her, to remind her where the bath towels were or just to tell her how happy I was to have her here, but the slight echo of her words in the hall stopped me.

"Is this what happened to our mother?"

I froze as I heard those words. How could she say that? Our mother . . . oh God, our mother had been crazy. She was psychotic and unbalanced, and it killed me to hear Charlie say that.

All my life, my greatest fear has been that I would turn out like our mother once I had a child. But I hadn't. Far from it. Grace had changed me in more ways than I could ever imagine. She'd made me into a better person.

So, why would Charlie say that?

CHAPTER SIX

I curled up on the couch in the loft area and waited for Charlie. I tried to sit still, to pretend that her comment earlier didn't bother me. It was hard, though.

The loft area had recently been cleaned and purged, I think. Nina must have been in a decluttering mood, because all the blankets and books I had left on the couch and coffee table had been replaced with magazines.

"Sorry I took so long. The hot water felt so good." Charlie set a large box down beside the couch and plopped down beside me.

"What's that?" I couldn't take my eyes off the old cardboard box. In thick black marker were the words *Old Stuff–Don't Throw Away* written on both the top and side of the box that I could see.

Charlie shrugged. She settled on the couch, curling her legs beneath her. "Just some stuff I thought you might like to go through later. Did you have lunch?"

"Just some toast. I wasn't too hungry." I was really curious about what was inside the box. What kind of old stuff would Charlie want to look through? "Did you let Marcus know you were here, safe and sound?" I caught the way she hardly spoke about him earlier. Another thing that was . . . off. Charlie and Marcus first met in South America more than three years ago and had been inseparable since then. It had been a foregone conclusion that they'd get married, and frankly, I was surprised they weren't by now.

She twisted her engagement ring around her finger before she gave a little shrug of her shoulders.

"We're kind of . . . taking a break."

I didn't say anything, but the questions I wanted to ask her swirled in my head. A break? What kind of break? She was still wearing her ring, so it must not be a permanent one.

"He gave me an ultimatum and, well, we both know how I respond to those." She rolled her eyes.

"Shut up." Charlie was known for her stubbornness.

Charlie shrugged before picking up an *Oprah* magazine and leafing through it.

"What did he want?" I couldn't believe I had to drag this out of her.

"A baby."

The way she said it made it sound like the world was going to end, like it was the worst thing that ever could have happened to her. And I understood; I really did. I once thought the same thing, until I held Grace in my arms.

"It's not as bad as we thought, Charlie. It's really not." It was better. Heaven instead of the hell we'd envisioned.

"You don't know that." Her lips tightened in defiance.

"I do. Look at me. I'm fine." I leaned forward and gently touched her knee.

She jerked it away from me.

"Diane, we made a pact with Mags, remember? That if we were ever to have children, we would only adopt. Remember?"

"We were kids. We had no idea what we were promising." I leaned back and prepared myself for this conversation. I knew where it was leading, and as much as I hated it, my little sister needed it. I somehow needed to show her that things were different.

"Maybe I didn't. But you did. And Mags. Mags knew. She lived through it with us." Charlie sighed. "I thought Marcus understood that. He said he did. He said he was okay with adoption and he still is, but . . . he wants his own natural child too. And I can't. You know that,

I know that. I thought he did as well." She played with the ring on her finger again. "I thought we could have it all. Like you and Brian did."

"Have."

"What?" She glanced up and looked at me in confusion.

"Have. You said 'did.' You want what Brian and I have," I corrected her.

"Diane—"

"No. I get it," I interrupted. "Trust me. I thought what we had was enough. But with Grace, so much has changed. For the better. When I was pregnant, I thought my world had ended. I even thought about abortion. But Brian convinced me to let go of the past and to give our future a chance, and I'm so glad I did. Just because our mother couldn't cope—"

"Couldn't cope?" This time it was Charlie's turn to interrupt me. "She had postpartum psychosis, Diane. It was more than just not coping. She didn't smother our brother and then kill herself just because she couldn't cope. Are you kidding me?" She jumped up from the couch and paced the floor of the loft. "No, don't answer that. You're kidding yourself if you think that's true."

Her hands clenched at her sides while I just sat there, unable to reply. I didn't want to go there. She knew that. We didn't talk about what our mother did. It was how we coped. How I still coped.

"Charlie." I licked my dry lips and tried to think of something reassuring to say. "Charlie, things are different now. Back then, there was no help for Mom, but there is now. If, God forbid, this were to happen to us, that we would . . . you know, that we couldn't . . ." I couldn't say the words.

"Go crazy? Lose our minds? Experience not just depression but a life-altering disease that could have us killing our child? Is that what you're trying to say?" Charlie spat out the words, her face an ugly mask of anger and disdain.

"I will not kill Grace!" Anger bubbled up inside at the idea that I would do anything as horrid as that.

Charlie stopped her pacing and dropped to her knees. Her shoulders sagged as she stared at me.

"Of course you wouldn't. But what about me? What if I killed my child? Christopher was her third child, our baby brother. What if we were the ones to drive Mom over the edge? What if it was too much for her to take care of all of us? God knows she had enough on her hands with an alcoholic husband. Maybe we were too much?" Charlie bowed her head. "If I have Marcus's baby, I wouldn't be with Doctors Without Borders anymore. I'd be home, alone, raising our child. What if it's too much for me?"

I dropped down to the floor beside her and grabbed hold of her hand.

"We are not our mother. Just because it happened to her doesn't mean it will happen to us. It doesn't. Mags was wrong." I gripped her hand hard while my body shook. From anger or fear, I wasn't sure.

Charlie lifted her head and stared at me. I could see the words forming on her lips, as if she had something she wanted to say, but she stopped herself. Her body deflated and I knew, in that instant, that something drastically had changed between us. She pulled her hand away from mine and gripped her knees.

"I don't think she was. I've seen a lot of cases of postpartum depression and psychosis. There's so much the medical community doesn't know about this disease. They don't know if it's hereditary, in the genes, or just a hormonal imbalance. But I'm not willing to risk my child's life. I'm just not." She stared at me, tears glistening in her eyes. I saw the questions there; I knew what she was asking.

"You know better than anyone that I didn't want to ever have children. And I'll be the first to admit that I fought it every step of the way until the end. But, Charlie, those last few weeks while I was on bed rest, something changed inside of me. There was only her and me, no other distractions, no matter how hard I tried to find some. She was always there, inside of me. I started to long to feel her move; I tried to see if I could feel the outline of her hands or her feet." I covered my stomach with my hand and spread my fingers, recalling the memory of those flutters I'd felt. "I know this sounds . . . not like me, but there was one moment, just one, when I swear there was a connection between us. "Her hand had pushed up on my belly and I could see," my eyes closed as I remembered, "the imprint so clearly, that I knew, the moment I laid my hand on top of hers, that I would do anything to not risk her life."

I eased back to lean against the couch. "I knew right from the beginning I would need a nanny." Even if I never told Brian that, it was as if he knew somehow. "Someone to help me with Grace, someone who could see . . . the signs, you know? Just in case."

Charlie leaned toward me. The baby monitor on the coffee table crackled and then I heard Grace's tiny whimpers. When I went to reach for it, Charlie grabbed my hand.

"Would you know the signs of postpartum psychosis if your nanny wasn't around?"

I shook Charlie's hand off as I stood.

"Of course I would. Trust me, I've got my doctor on speed dial. But I'm fine." I wrapped my arms around my sister and pulled her close. "Grace is everything I don't deserve. She's my little angel, my world. I would do anything to keep her safe. Anything. That's what being a mother is all about. Keeping our children safe."

I let go and stepped back. Grace's whimpers stopped and the only sound I heard was the soft cadence of her breathing.

"You know"—I stared at Charlie—"Mags once told me that's what our mother did. She was protecting us the only way she knew how. I didn't understand it at the time, but I do now. She killed herself to keep us safe."

———

I wrinkled my nose in disgust at the musty smell as I opened the box Charlie had brought for me to look at. I rubbed my fingers on my pants to clean the film of dust that came from the cardboard. Where had she kept this thing? It must have been at the back of a storage locker, long forgotten about.

I turned the box around and saw more writing: *Diane's Journals/ Childhood Items.* My hands shook as I pushed the box away from me. Where had she gotten this? I hadn't seen it in years.

Our talk earlier today all made sense now. Charlie brought this over because she needed reassurance. I could give her that with what was inside this box.

Shortly after we moved in with Aunt Mags, she'd taken us to see a counselor. We didn't really say much at the time; Charlie literally didn't say anything at all. Not for six months. She'd been the one to find our mother first.

God, I hated thinking about that time. I'd worked so hard to forget about it, to lock it away in a tiny box within my mind. Dredging it up now hurt. But inside this box were the answers, for myself and for Charlie.

I pulled the box closer and opened it. The first item on top was an old pink sweater my mom used to wear around the house, a cardigan she'd knitted while she was pregnant with me. I remembered her telling me she used to sing to me while she knitted the sweater, and then when I was older and would wake in the middle of the night from bad dreams, she'd wrap me up in it and rub my back until I fell asleep again.

Even though I knew any smell that I'd hoped would have lingered from my mom would be gone by now, I rubbed the wool between my fingers and brought it up to my nose.

There were other things inside the box, hidden beneath this sweater. My journals, the pipe my father used to keep on a shelf in our living room, and the baby blanket I'd found discarded beneath Christopher's crib the day he died. Things I knew I needed to keep but never really wanted to see again.

I picked up the soft baby-blue blanket that my mom used to wrap Christopher in. I remembered him being a small baby who cried a lot. Mom used to bundle him up tight in the blanket and rock him to sleep. His bedroom had been on the other side of Charlie's and mine and I could still hear the creak of the old rocking chair in my dreams, along with his cries.

It was why I hated to hear Grace cry.

I used to wonder whether our lives would have been different if our father had stuck around after everything happened. Days after my mother killed herself, he dropped Charlie and me off at Aunt Mags's with a suitcase full of our stuff. We sat in the car while he knocked on her door. I remember him pointing at us and then at himself. I have no idea what he said, but he handed her keys and then came back to us. He opened our door, got our suitcase out of the trunk, and then before we even had the chance to walk into the house, he was gone.

We never heard from him again.

It was Aunt Mags who cleaned out the apartment before the landlord confiscated all our stuff. She let us pick out the things we wanted to keep the most while she packed our clothes and the rest of our toys. I chose my mother's sweater, my dad's pipe, and Christopher's blanket. Charlie took a picture of all of us after Christopher had been born.

Wrapped inside the baby blanket were journals. My journals. The ones Mags gave to me to write down everything that I couldn't say. I would sit in my bedroom for hours writing in these books. I bet I filled more than a dozen of them in the first year we lived with Mags. I didn't keep them all. In fact, I thought I had gotten rid of all the journals when I went to college, only to find out that Mags had rescued some of the earlier ones from the garbage. She knew one day I'd want to read them, to remember, and maybe to heal.

If it weren't for Charlie, I wouldn't be doing this. These weren't memories I wanted to lose myself in. I was okay with keeping them padlocked in my mind.

But I hated to see her so sad. She belonged with Marcus. His strengths built up her weakness and vice versa. She was happier with him, and I didn't like to see her so torn.

I placed the journals on the ground and refolded the blanket before placing it back in the box. Later tonight I'd go through my memories and reawaken the old demons.

CHAPTER SEVEN

"What a nice surprise to finally meet Charlie." Nina poured me a cup of tea as we had our nightly chat before bed.

I played with the pills on the table, rolling them in circles before placing them one by one on my tongue and swallowing.

"Did you two have a nice talk?" I asked.

I'd overheard the low murmur of their voices as I rocked Grace to sleep earlier. I couldn't make out their entire conversation, but I got the gist of it. And I didn't like what I heard.

"She's worried about you." Nina looked at me out of the corner of her eye.

"I know. But she doesn't need to be."

"Of course she does." Nina raised her teacup. "She's your sister. It's her right to be worried."

"You do realize she's my younger sister, right? I'm the one who's supposed to be taking care of her. She looks like a mess." Even after her shower, Charlie had looked like she needed to sleep for at least a week. "Can you do some extra baking while she's here? She's lost a lot of weight since I last saw her."

Nina scribbled something down in her notebook. That blasted notebook. One day, I was going to lay my hands on it and read what she wrote down every day about me.

"I noticed the pile of notebooks on your desk earlier." Nina laid down her pen and glanced behind her to where my desk was.

My lips pursed. I didn't want to talk about them. Not right now. Maybe after I'd read them. I was only ten years old when I wrote in the first journal, and who knows what I wrote then. The last thing I needed was for Nina to psychoanalyze me.

"I want to go into work for a few hours tomorrow. I know it's not on the schedule, but will you be around to watch Grace?"

The frown on Nina's face said it all.

"It's just for a few hours, I promise."

"Don't you think you should spend time with your sister? That's why she's here, after all."

I winced. She was right.

"I know, but . . ." I really couldn't think of a valid excuse.

"Did something happen between you and Charlie? Is that why you'd rather go into work than spend time with her?"

I shrugged my shoulders.

"That's not an answer, Diane."

I hated when Nina admonished me like that. It wasn't just how she looked at me, with disappointment in her eyes. But it was her tone and the little sigh she gave before she asked me the question.

I wasn't sure how I was supposed to react with Charlie now, after everything that happened yesterday. Nor was I sure that she really wanted to spend time with me and Grace. Other than her holding Grace when she first arrived, she'd shown no real interest in my daughter, and I wasn't sure how to handle that. I knew it was in large part due to her own personal fears and her engagement with Marcus, but still.

"I feel like I need to show Charlie that I haven't changed, that I'm still the big sister I've always been."

Nina sipped at her tea and watched me from over the rim of the cup. "So you think you're showing her this, how?"

"I'm not." I shook my head. "But I see it in her eyes, the way she watches me when she thinks I'm not looking."

"What is she looking for?" Nina reached for her pen and had it poised over the notebook.

"To see if I've gone crazy. Like our mother did. I know she is, and I don't know how to convince her I'm fine."

Nina stood up, walked over to my desk, and grabbed the journal from the top of the pile. I stiffened at her actions. What was she doing?

"Do you think you've gone crazy?" She sat back down and placed the journal between us.

I fidgeted in my seat, unable to stay still. My arms were going numb so I flexed them, dropping them to my side and raising them over and over while wiggling my fingers. Nina just sat there and watched me.

"No, I don't think so." I scratched the top of my itchy eyelid and then rubbed my ear. All of a sudden I was itchy all over.

"You don't know or you don't think so?" Nina picked up her pen again.

"Stop writing about me in your notebook!" I blurted.

Nina's hand stilled. She set down the pen, closed the book, and folded her hands on her lap.

"What makes you think I was writing about you? Perhaps I was making a grocery list for all the baked goods I now have to make."

Embarrassed, I bowed my head and glanced at her out of the corner of my eye. I felt like I'd just gotten my hand slapped, like a small child reaching for a cookie after being told no. Except I wasn't a child and I didn't need to feel that way.

"Diane, I couldn't help but notice the journals on your desk." Nina picked up the book but didn't open it.

Part of me was perturbed that she would go through my things, but another part of me expected it and was a bit relieved she'd done so. Maybe I could discuss this with her, talk about some of the symptoms my mother experienced, and find a way to discount Charlie's fears.

"My mother went . . . crazy after she gave birth to our baby brother. Back then"—I shrugged and stared down at the table, unwilling to see the reaction on Nina's face—"there really was no way to get her any help or even realize she needed help."

"How old were you?"

"Not very old; it was before my tenth birthday." I shook my head. "Young enough to not really understand what was going on. Charlie and I had just come home from school. Normally, our mom would be there to walk us home, but after Christopher was born, she had a neighbor meet us at school instead. Charlie was the one who found them. I'll never forget her screams." I shuddered at the memory. "Never."

"What happened?" Her voice was tender; I ignored the fact that her hand inched its way back to her notebook.

"Go ahead and write . . . I know you want to." I leaned forward and pushed it toward her.

I couldn't believe I was going to share what happened with her. Brian knew, and I was sure he'd mentioned something to Nina before he left for London, but other than Charlie, Aunt Mags, and the counselor I saw during those early years, I hadn't told anyone else. No one else needed to know. Walter knew I'd lost my mother at an early age and that she'd died with my younger brother, but that was it.

I felt safe with Nina. I trusted her with my life. With Grace's life.

I licked my lips and cleared my throat.

"She was in her rocking chair and Christopher was in her lap. His head was cushioned on her arm but his lips and face were all blue. On the side table was a glass of water and an empty pill bottle and a note. They said . . ." I winced at the pain as I struggled to swallow. "They said she suffocated him while she nursed him and then overdosed when she realized what she'd done." I tilted my head up to stare at the ceiling and blinked past the swell of tears in my eyes. I was not going to cry. I wasn't.

"Who's *they*, Diane?" Nina asked.

"The police. I can still hear Charlie's screams, you know. I wish . . . God, I wish I had gone to check on the baby first. It's what we did every day after school. We couldn't wait to see him. But they'd handed out little trees at school and I wanted to put mine in a cup of water so it wouldn't dry." I shook my head at the memory. "It's funny the things you remember, those details that really don't matter in the scheme of things."

"They do matter."

"We were only kids. We had no idea what happened. Our neighbor must have heard Charlie's screams, because she was the one to call the police. I remember one of the officers talking to his partner and calling my brother a victim. I was standing right beside him, beside Christopher; I refused to leave him. I kept my eyes on him, to see if his lips would move, to see if he would come back to life. I prayed while we waited, prayed that God would save him . . . and I waited. But God never answered. I told the officer his name was Christopher and that was the last thing I said for months."

Nina laid down her pen and crossed her legs.

"You didn't speak?"

I shook my head.

"Neither one of us did. Counselor said we were in shock and told our Aunt Mags to love us and once we felt safe, we'd talk. And we did. Eventually. It took Charlie six months.

"This is how we spoke." I picked up the journal and held it tight to my chest. "Between the two of us, I'm sure we went through fifty or more journals. Charlie was around six years old, and she couldn't print very well, so she'd draw lots of pictures. But I would spend hours writing. I'd lock myself away in our room with Mags and pour out all my thoughts, my questions, my dreams, in these books." I pressed the book harder into my chest and the edges dug into my breasts.

"What was on the note?"

The note. I shook my head. I didn't want to talk about the note. I'd tried to hide it beneath the mattress of Christopher's crib before anyone else saw it, but the neighbor caught me and snatched it from my fingers. She'd given it to the police officers, who'd then shown the note to my father. It was the look on his face, the despair, the confusion, and even a hint of hatred when he looked at both Charlie and me, that scared me the most. I think that was why it didn't surprise me when he'd dropped us off at Aunt Mags's and never returned.

He blamed us for what happened, and he was right.

It was our fault.

"You don't remember, or you don't want to talk about it?"

"It's not really that important," I hedged. I really didn't want to talk about it.

"So, why bring out the journals? Did Charlie want to see them or are you looking for something in particular?" Thankfully, she got the hint. That was one thing I loved about Nina. She knew when not to push. Although I had no doubt she'd try to get me to talk about it another way. Just like now, she kept going back to the journals.

"Charlie brought them." I motioned to the box I'd set to the side. "She asked if I would recognize the signs of postpartum psychosis, and I told her I would."

"But . . ."

"But I'm not so sure. I thought maybe the answers would be here, in my childish scribblings. Maybe I'd be able to recognize what happened to force my mom to kill our brother and then herself."

"Are you worried?"

Was I worried? Good question. Worried for Charlie, maybe. I wanted to reassure her that she wouldn't be alone, that I would be there for her. But that wasn't the whole truth either.

"Do you think you have postpartum psychosis, Diane? Are you trying to find symptoms you might share with your mother?"

Share. What a word. How did you share symptoms with someone who was dead? With someone who lived a different life from the one you led? Could I share these symptoms? I had one child. She had three. We were both basically single parents. But that's as far as the similarities went.

"No." There was a difference between my mother and me.

I would never harm Grace. Ever. No matter what. I would never place blame on her tiny little shoulders for something I couldn't handle. She was innocent, and I would do everything in my power to keep her that way.

"Then what are you looking for?" Nina gathered up our empty cups and placed them on the tray.

"Reassurance, maybe? That I would know what to look for, just in case."

Nina stood up and grabbed hold of the tray's handles.

"I won't ever let anything happen to you, Diane. I made you a promise that first day I came here. You are my priority. That includes your well-being, not only physically but mentally too. There's nothing I won't do for you." There was a determination to her stance. Her shoulders were pushed back and her knuckles whitened as she held the tray.

Relief washed over me at her words. I didn't realize how tense I was until I let out a deep breath. I wasn't sure what brought on such fierce devotion from Nina, but whatever it was, the journal dropped from my hands as I pushed myself out of my chair, grabbed the tray, and set it down before putting my arms around her. I held on as if she were my lifeline, and to be honest, I thought she was.

"We'll get through this," Nina murmured as she patted my back. "I promise you we'll get through this."

I didn't answer her. I wasn't sure what she was referring to, unless she knew something I didn't, but at that moment it didn't matter.

Nina was more to me than just a nurse or a nanny. She was like a mother to me and I never wanted to let go of that.

Never.

CHAPTER EIGHT

Brian

March 2013

Brian paced back and forth in his office, sidestepping the layers of network cables and boxes stacked here and there full of computer cords. He practiced his speech for the meeting in ten minutes, repeating it until he got it the way he wanted it to sound. He wiped at the sweat dripping down his face with a napkin he'd found shoved in his desk drawer and berated himself for being so nervous.

It wasn't like they were about to fire him. He'd more than proven his dedication to the firm throughout the years. Still, he'd hardly slept last night, planning for each and every contingency he could think of: who could replace him, who would prove to be more of a threat than he'd anticipated, and the perfect person to recommend in his stead. If things went according to plan, he'd be providing the firm with a well-thought-out plan.

There was really no other option.

His phone buzzed on his desk. He glanced down to find a text from Diane.

I think it's a mistake. You love to travel. It's always been your dream.

Brian grunted. Of course she did. But he'd made her a promise. She made her point last night during one of their many arguments when she'd mentioned that it was easy for him to want a child when *she* was the one sacrificing everything. He'd countered that she wasn't the only one sacrificing. He was giving up his dream of traveling, something he loved to do more than anything else. But it was worth it. That wasn't even a question. He'd willingly give up all the experiences he'd had over the years in the various countries where they'd set up offices for this chance to have a baby.

You gave me the options. This is my choice. I love you. Brian texted back.

There was a knock on the door. Brian pocketed his phone while Nicole Murray, the lead administrative assistant for his department, opened the door.

"They're ready for you."

Brian squared his shoulders. "Thanks." He walked past her and down the hallway, passing cubicles upon cubicles where those who worked in his department all raised their heads to watch him.

The boardroom sat at the end of the hallway with its tinted windows. Any and all meetings were held in an array of boardrooms similar to this one on their floor. Brian remembered the first time he'd sat in on a meeting in this room, having just started with the firm and feeling very nervous. Back then, upper management held an allure of mystery to him. Now the endless meetings he endured were monotonous and time-consuming.

Brian pushed open the door and smiled at those sitting around the table. Nicole followed him, heading to the refreshment table and pouring him a coffee. Brian pulled out his chair and settled down. He smiled in thanks to Nicole as she placed a cup in front of him and then took her seat beside other administrators from the firm who sat along the wall, notebooks in their hands.

Monday mornings were office meetings, where the upper echelon of the company met with those in management beneath them. A few years ago, the meeting agendas had changed so that technology discussions happened in the last half of the meetings, leaving Brian free to deal with any issues that had arisen over the weekend in their firms around the globe.

"Brian." Timothy Wainright, the firm's COO, nodded in greeting. "We were just discussing the new office in London. We've upped the time frame and would like everything set up before the new year. We have a team in place there to help you with the transition."

"That's not leaving me much time. I thought a March date had been decided?" Brian's stomach knotted up.

His boss, Will Harper, the firm's CEO, leaned forward. "Is there a problem? Nine months should leave you plenty of time. You set up the Dubai office in six."

"Well, ah." Brian gulped. He couldn't recall a single word of the memorized speech he'd prepared. "Nine months is plenty of time, but I'd like to suggest that I have Marie lead this transition. It should be seamless, and a good experience for her."

There was a slight shuffling of papers on the table before Will Harper.

"As long as you are overseeing her to ensure there are no complications, I don't have a problem with that."

Brian breathed a sigh of relief and couldn't believe how easy that had been. No explanations, no excuses. He should have known better. It wasn't common knowledge that Diane was pregnant, but a few people did know. Will was one of them.

The rest of the meeting progressed as usual, but when Brian rose from his chair at the end, Will asked him to stay behind. He glanced back toward Nicole but Will shook his head. That response had Brian's stomach twisting in knots. Something was up. If Nicole wasn't included then it didn't bode well.

Brian took the seat opposite Will and waited for the man to look up from his phone.

"Everything okay at home?" Will finally asked.

Brian rubbed the back of his neck and tried to find a comfortable position in the chair. "Everything's fine. And you? How are your kids?"

A smile crossed Will's face. His wife just gave birth to their third child a few months ago. "The house is in chaos with the baby again. Mindi's doing great, though; she was made to be a mother."

Brian forced a smile onto his face and nodded. He wished he could say the same thing about his wife. Maybe in time, those motherly instincts just became second nature. Maybe once the morning sickness went away.

"I wanted to talk about Marie and your decision to have her lead the setup of the new London office." Will pushed the stack of papers forward and folded his hands together. "How much of this decision is based on the need to further Marie's career and how much based on your need to be home with Diane right now?"

Brian licked his lips and adjusted his glasses. Will knew him too well. They'd known each other for years, and it was Will who'd landed him this job, through a personal recommendation. Brian couldn't really hide things from him.

"It's a little rough right now," he admitted. "But you know Diane." He shrugged. He wasn't about to admit just how rough things were at home.

Will nodded. "Mindi's hormones were all over the place with this last pregnancy. It's not easy on them. I'm okay with Marie going over, but I need to know that you'll be there if we need you."

Brian nodded. Of course he would. He just hoped it wouldn't come to that.

"Marie is good. She's taken on projects like this with the last company she was with. I'll make sure that she's up to speed on our processes, but I wouldn't have recommended her if I didn't believe in her." Brian spoke with pride. He'd been the one to find Marie languishing at a smaller firm, where her talents were sadly ignored. She had a brilliant mind, caught on fast, and, much to his surprise, was one of the best hackers he knew. She'd saved his butt a few times when their firewalls had been breached and she'd located the hole before he did.

"I trust you, Brian. I just needed to make sure. This new London office is a huge score for us." Will gathered his papers and stood. "Tim is still disappointed that you turned down the offer to head that team for us."

Brian shrugged. "Moving there isn't an option. With Diane's new role and now a baby on the way, even the commute wouldn't work. But I'm honored he wanted me for that job."

Turning down that promotion had been hard. When he'd mentioned it to Diane at the time, her promotion was to happen within a month and she wouldn't even consider the thought of moving. She'd suggested he commute, something many of his friends in their field did, but being away from her for any length of time always had him in knots. And now, with her pregnant, it wasn't an option he was even willing to consider.

"Personally, I'm glad you turned him down. I'd hate to lose you here. But I'd like you to be open to the possibility of some future travel for us before the baby arrives. You can accrue some overtime and then take extra days off once the little one is here."

Brian didn't say anything. He'd rather not travel at all. He needed to be there for Diane, to show his support, and to make sure she was okay. She'd never admitted it, but deep down, he knew that the source of her hesitation to have a baby for so many years was because of what happened with her mother. He knew she was worried the same thing might happen with her.

Truth be told, so was he. Losing Diane was not an option. He'd do anything in his power to make sure that never happened.

———

Brian stood at the stove and sampled the sauce bubbling in the pot. Diane was working late again, and he had a craving for homemade spaghetti instead of ordering in like they normally did. In their early years, they used to work side by side in the kitchen. Brian missed those days. They used to take culinary weekends away with a local cooking school until their schedules became too full. A few years ago, they had spent a week in Napa Valley for their anniversary. Maybe they should do something like that again, before the baby came.

He sprinkled a little more salt and then added some fresh-ground pepper when the sound of the key in the lock caught his attention. He lowered the flame, set the lid on the pot, and wiped his hands on the black dish towel he'd flung over his shoulder.

Not for the first time, he thought that this condo of theirs wasn't meant for a family. He could count on one hand the number of couples with small children in their building. Most of the time, people moved out once they had kids, and he didn't blame them. One look at their unit—particularly, one look at their monochromatic kitchen with stainless-steel appliances—and you knew it had been created for entertaining, not the sticky fingers that were sure to follow once their little tyke started walking.

A smile spread across Brian's face. He could picture the piles of dump trucks and action hero figures on the floor. Funny how he was already assuming they were having a boy. But what if they were having a girl? Would the house be filled with pink blankets and decorations? He shook his head. No, not in this place.

"I'm home," Diane called out as she closed the door behind her. "Please tell me you're making what I think you're making." There was a thump, which Brian knew was her purse being dropped on the floor, followed by another two thumps; this time, her shoes.

"I was inspired to do some fresh Italian cooking when I got home. Hope that's okay?" The tiredness in her voice concerned him. She was working too hard lately. He waited for her to come into the kitchen, refilling his wineglass with a merlot and pouring sparkling water into another glass.

"Sounds great. I'm just going to get changed. Be down in a minute."

Brian took a step to follow her and then stopped. Considering her mood in the last few days, staying downstairs might be the safest option for him.

He stuck his iPod on its base and turned the volume on low while he pulled out a large bread knife and sliced the French loaf he'd picked up at the bakery on his way home. He'd made a butter-garlic mixture earlier. All he needed to do was toss the salad and stick the bread in the oven, and dinner would be ready.

While Brian worked, he also cleaned up after himself. As the bread toasted, he wiped down the counter, set the table, and even lit the candles he'd found in the china cabinet. A smile bloomed on his face at his efforts. It wasn't dinner at Luigi's, their favorite place to dine, but it was elegant and even slightly romantic. Fingers crossed that Diane appreciated his efforts.

"I forgot to tell you, my talk at work went well," Brian yelled up the stairs.

"That's good."

The timer on the stove buzzed and Brian hurried over, almost catching his foot on the barstool as he skidded across the hardwood floor. The last thing he wanted was to have the scent of burned garlic bread in the air.

A slight noise from upstairs told him that Diane was coming down. He pulled out the bread, left the oven door ajar to let out the heat, and went to stand at the bottom of stairs. He looked at all the hardwood flooring in the house, even on the stairway, and immediately pictured his little child slipping down the stairs or sliding on the floor while trying to crawl. He tried to picture toys littering the floor, but the idea of toys in their ultramodern house seemed out of place.

He liked the idea of moving into a house designed to be a home filled with childish laughter and even the barking of a family pet. Something softer. He shook his head at that thought. He couldn't believe he used the word *soft* to describe his future home. Next thing he knew, he'd be looking at minivans and booking playdates with other stay-at-home dads.

Brian swallowed hard. Where did that thought come from? Since when did he want to be a stay-at-home dad? He scoffed at the idea.

"What's wrong?"

Brian glanced up to find Diane standing at the bottom stair in front of him, a concerned look on her face.

He shook his head, hoping to dislodge the idea of him being *that* type of man, and forced a smile.

"Nothing. Ready to eat?" He held out his hand and pulled her into his arms when she reached out. He loved holding her close, the feel of her body against his, knowing that in these small moments, there was nothing but them in their lives.

She pulled back, her face scrunched up.

"Brian." She covered her nose with her hand and shook her head.

"Oh, no, is it the garlic bread?"

She nodded her head before running toward the bathroom. Guilt ate at him while he listened to her retching.

Brian searched the kitchen, trying to think of what he could do to get rid of the smell. Obviously, all his hard work on the homemade garlic butter was wasted. He wrapped the bread in napkins since it was hot and threw it out in the garbage in their garage. He then went in and swung open the door off their dining area to their back porch, since there was a nice breeze. He hoped it would dispel the scent and Diane could at least enjoy the spaghetti.

"God, I hate this." Diane rubbed her face as she walked into the kitchen.

Brian handed her the water he'd poured earlier. Her nose was still scrunched up.

"I thought morning sickness only happened, well . . . in the morning?"

The heated look Diane threw his way as she sipped her water told him otherwise.

"I'm sorry." He didn't know what else to say.

Diane slumped down on a barstool. "I'm sorry about the garlic bread."

Brian moved behind her and gently rubbed her back. She hung her head low and he worked at getting the kinks out of her neck and shoulders.

"It's okay. I burned it anyway," he lied. "Is it this bad during the day?"

Diane moaned. He took that as a yes.

"You have some vacation time coming. Why don't you take some days off?"

"I can't. Too many meetings booked in the next month."

Brian ground his thumbs into a tight spot on her shoulder. "Don't you think you should slow down the pace a little?"

Brian's hands fell as Diane leaned forward and twisted to look at him.

"I can't. You know that. Just because I'm pregnant doesn't give me any leeway at work."

Brian sat on the stool beside her. "I don't want you to run yourself ragged, that's all. It's not good for you or the baby."

Diane shook her head.

"I'm just worried about you." He knew she wouldn't give herself any downtime even though she was pregnant.

"Maybe once I'm further along and people know, but for now, I can't."

He bit his tongue to keep from responding and instead focused on filling their plates with noodles, until he thought about what she'd just said.

"Wait a minute." His hand stilled above the pot of sauce. "You haven't told Walter?"

Diane shook her head.

This surprised him. From the way Walter had spoken at the party, he figured she'd told him.

"Does anyone know?" He waited to see if she'd have the decency to look at him, but she didn't.

Brian's shoulders slumped. He didn't understand why she was so hesitant.

She got up from the stool and rounded the island to stand beside him. "I just want to wait. To keep this as our secret for now." Her arms wound around his waist and she laid her head on his back.

"For how long?" How long did she want to deny the changes coming their way? Pretty soon, she would start showing. Then what?

"Until I know I can cope."

Brian linked his fingers through Diane's. He knew in that moment that he really had no idea what this was doing to her.

Her fingers wrenched from his as she ran out of the kitchen, her words filling the silence in their kitchen.

"God, I hate this," she said, repeating her earlier sentiment.

———

He couldn't believe the amount of information available online for men with expectant spouses. Diane had barely eaten at dinner and then headed upstairs without another word. He knew when he heard the water going that she was having a bath. He had watched her visibly wilt during dinner and it worried him. After cleaning up the kitchen, he grabbed his laptop, sat down on the couch, and decided it was time for him to take some action. He did a quick search, narrowing down what he was looking for, and found a blog post on how husbands could support their pregnant wives.

Listen. Check.

Help. Diane wasn't a woman who accepted help too easily. Besides, what was he supposed to do, hold her hair out of the way while she puked? No, that wouldn't go over very well. The first time he had found her hunched over the toilet, she demanded he leave and then slammed the door closed with her foot.

Be at her beck and call. He doubted she'd be one of those women who woke up with a burger-and-milk-shake craving at two in the morning, but if she did, he'd get it for her.

Take her on a date. What a great idea. Brian pulled open his calendar and checked to find a night when they would both be home. They used to schedule a date night every two weeks but somehow that idea fell to the side once things started picking up at work for both of them. He'd bring it up after her bath and see if maybe there was a movie she wanted to see.

Be eager. Brian sighed. He was more eager for this baby than she was. He was sure that would change; it had to. The motherly instinct would kick in and then he'd feel left out by the bond between her and the baby. He pictured her, how her body would change as the months progressed. Right now she was thin, working out religiously every morning before she headed into work. He couldn't wait to see a little belly on her, and then watch it grow. Feel their child's movement beneath his hands. She was going to glow, be even more beautiful than he ever thought possible.

Show a little romance. He'd show her a lot of romance, if it would make her happy. He used to buy her flowers weekly, but now it was once a month. He overheard her complain to a friend on the phone once that the thrill of receiving flowers waned when they arrived all the time. But maybe he could buy her other things, or even do other things. Romance wasn't about how much money he could spend; it was about showing her he loved her. When they were first married, he used to be inventive, proud of himself for thinking outside the box when it came to being romantic. He used to write her little love notes and leave them lying around their home.

Book a spa treatment for her. She already did this herself. She had a weekly appointment booked for a massage, manicure, and all that other girly stuff.

Help her relax. That was the key. But how? She was all strung out, tense from everything happening at work. He'd almost flipped when he saw the bruising on her back and shoulders last week after her massage. Diane was used to stress and normally handled it well, but what would it do to the baby? It couldn't be good for her body. He jotted down on the notepad beside him, *Look for relaxation techniques other than massage.*

Book a cleaning service. Brian glanced around. Their house was spotless, thanks to a cleaning service Diane had had come in for the past few years now. Scratch that off the list.

Treat her to some great maternity clothes. Now, this one he could do. Diane loved to shop. There had to be some upscale maternity shops nearby. *Maternity gift card*, he wrote down.

Let her know she's beautiful. Another easy thing to do. His wife was drop-dead gorgeous; always had been and always would be. Did he tell her enough? He thought he did. But knowing her, he probably could tell her more. It all depended on her mood swings. One day she'd accuse him of not being romantic enough and then another time tell him he'd gone overboard.

He shut the lid to his laptop and stood, stretching the kinks out of his back. Now that he had a list, something to work from to help Diane through her pregnancy, he could relax. He grabbed a beer from the kitchen and took a long swig, enjoying the cool sensation of the liquid flowing down his throat.

Maybe he'd go up and see if Diane needed help drying off. He couldn't think of a more perfect way to end the evening, especially one that didn't start off as he'd anticipated.

CHAPTER NINE

The buzzing of a phone startled Brian from a dream full of crying babies. He rolled over and wrapped his arms around Diane, only to have her push him away. Brian snaked his arm over her waist anyway and snuggled up against her backside.

"Hello." Diane wiggled out of his grasp and struggled to sit up in bed.

Brian glanced at the alarm clock and groaned. It was three o'clock in the morning. Who on earth would call at this time? He plopped his head back down on his pillow and threw his arm over his eyes as Diane turned on her bedside lamp.

"Walter, slow down. It's too early."

Brian lifted his arm briefly as Diane swung her legs out of bed and sat with her back to him. She leaned forward, her head in her hands, and thankfully blocked some of the light.

"Why is he calling?" Brian managed to mumble. Diane waved one of her hands in the air, her signal for him to leave her alone, so he rolled over and pulled the blanket over his head.

"At least shut the light off," he grumbled. She must have heard him, because moments later the light switched off. The slight shuffle of her feet and then the soft click of their en suite door left him alone in their room.

Brian tried to listen, but Diane's voice was muted so all he heard were whispers. Why was Walter calling her at this hour? Why couldn't he just leave her alone? Wasn't it enough that he got her during the day; did he have to steal Brian's nights with her as well?

Water ran from the sink and the door opened. A sliver of light shone into their room.

"Okay, Walter. I'll be right there. No, no, you don't need to do anything. I've got it covered."

Brian rose up on his elbow and winced as Diane opened the door farther.

"Sorry," she whispered. "I just need to grab some clothes."

"You're kidding me, right?" Brian rubbed his eyes and yawned.

He heard her rummage through her drawers and then the slight clink of hangers from the closet as she grabbed clothes.

"Walter needs me."

That caught Brian's attention. It was the inflection in her voice, as if his needing her were all that mattered to her.

"So he just snaps his fingers and you come running?"

"Brian." She sighed heavily. "There's an emergency with one of our overseas clients. The server is down, no one can get ahold of Neil, and so one of the front desk workers called Walter in a panic."

"And you're his go-to gal even at"—Brian glanced at the clock again—"this ungodly hour. Must be nice. Do you need help?" If no one could get ahold of Neil, maybe he could help troubleshoot. It wouldn't be the first time he'd helped in a pinch.

"No, Neil showed me what to do if something like this happened."

"Are you sure?"

"If I wanted your help, I'd ask, okay?"

Brian kept his mouth shut. She didn't need to bite his head off; all he did was offer to help. She'd been like this all night.

He'd come up earlier to help Diane dry off, only to be told to leave her alone. So, he'd gone back downstairs, poured himself another glass of merlot, and watched television until he knew she would be asleep. Every time he'd tried to cuddle with her in the night she pulled away.

He was surprised when she sat down on the edge of the bed and played with his hair.

"I'm sorry. I appreciate the offer, I really do. But the last time you came in and saved the day for Neil, Walter held it over his head for months." She leaned down and placed a kiss on his forehead. "Try to get some sleep."

"Only if you will. You need it more than me." He rubbed at his eyes, knowing she'd say no, and considered his options. His alarm would go off in a few hours. He could try falling back asleep or he could get up and head to the gym a bit earlier than normal.

"You know I can't."

Brian sighed. "Of course not. You would never think of saying no to Walter. Doesn't matter that you're pregnant and that it's time you maybe put yourself first instead of him. No, you'll just suffer, while he gets all the glory from your hard work." He rubbed his head. "God, sometimes I hate your job."

"What is wrong with you?" Diane pulled back and threw up her hands. "What happened to the caring and supportive husband who also gets three a.m. phone calls from his boss and has to go into work? I'm not an invalid, Brian; I'm not made of glass."

Brian blinked. What was wrong with *him*? She really had to ask him that?

"No, but you're pregnant, Diane, or have you forgotten that? It's not just you that you have to worry about anymore; it's our baby growing inside of you."

"That doesn't mean my life has to change." Diane turned her back on him and left their bedroom.

He couldn't believe she'd walk away from him like that. He followed her, throwing on a pair of boxers, and grabbed his robe from the hook on the door.

"I can't believe you're even arguing with me about this," he said once he reached the kitchen.

Diane stood at the sink where she was drinking a glass of water. She put the glass down on the counter and turned toward him, hands on her hips.

"Me? You're the one being a Neanderthal. What do you expect of me? I can't rearrange my life just because I'm pregnant. I know it's what you think I should do, but I won't. I can't. That's not who I am. I'm a businesswoman, Brian, with a promising career ahead of me, one that I've worked really hard for. I'm not going to allow this"—she placed her hand on her stomach for a split second—"to change who I am."

Her eyes blazed with fire as she spat out the words Brian couldn't believe he was hearing.

"Change you?"

Diane's hand shot up to cover her mouth as her eyes widened. "I'm scared, Brian. I'm just scared. I don't want . . ." she whispered.

"This? Our baby? Is that what you don't want?" Brian shook his head. He didn't believe that. He couldn't believe that. She was responding out of fear.

"Brian, I didn't mean that. You know that." Stricken, Diane stepped toward him, but Brian continued to shake his head. He held out his hand, as if to stop her.

"No. You did. We both know that. You're just being honest about it. That's . . ." He was about to say it was okay, but it wasn't. It really wasn't okay. He'd known in his heart that she felt this way, but he'd hoped he was wrong. Brian breathed deeply and struggled to clear his thoughts. The last thing Diane needed from him was judgment. He couldn't push her away; there was too much at stake.

"I know it's a shock and that it means things are going to change. But we talked about this. We wanted this, remember?" Brian dropped his hand, his shoulders sagging as Diane shook her head.

"No. You wanted this. I didn't. I never have, not really. I'm happy with our life. I'm finally where I want to be professionally; we're good, we're happy and successful, and I don't need anything else in my life."

Brian tried really hard to read past her words, to hear hope that she was afraid to admit in her voice. "You don't mean that. I know you don't."

Diane tugged at her lip with her teeth. "What if I do? What if I really do mean it?"

The weight of her words, the hesitation in her voice, it knocked the wind out of him. His knees gave out and Brian was forced to grab hold of the island counter for support. She couldn't possibly be saying what he was hearing.

Diane stepped close and laid her cold hand over his.

"Think about it, Brian. Having a baby now complicates things. I can't be a stay-at-home mom, you can't leave your position at work, and I don't want someone else raising our child. And what if . . ." Her voice dropped till he could barely make out the words. "My mother was in her early thirties when she had Christopher. I'm the same age as her." Her voice, meant to be soothing, only grated on his nerves until she whispered those last words.

He didn't know what he could do or even say to ease that fear. She was not her mother. What happened back then wasn't going to happen now. History would not repeat itself. He wouldn't let it.

He gathered his strength and stood. Now wasn't the time to discuss this. He forced himself to relax, to not visibly respond to what she was suggesting.

"Let's talk about this later, okay? What if we meet at Luigi's for a dinner? I'll leave work a little early. If we get there as they open, we'll have the place to ourselves, nice and quiet, and we can relax and really talk about what is happening to our lives."

Diane softened, her shoulders relaxed, and a soft smile appeared on her face. "We haven't really talked about this, have we?"

Brian shook his head.

Diane stepped closer and wrapped her arms around him. "Okay, that will be good."

Brian held her close as she laid her head on his shoulder.

He had a day. A day to figure out how to soothe his wife's fears, ease her mind, and prove to her that they could have their happily ever after.

———

Brian sat at the table and fiddled with the silverware.

Diane was late, but it didn't help that he'd arrived early either.

Today had been a complete waste. He wished he could blame it on being tired, but he was used to receiving calls in the middle of the night.

He just couldn't focus.

It didn't take him long to realize that when it came to their baby, Diane's needs and wants were all that mattered. She was going through an adjustment period. It was normal. It had to be. He couldn't imagine it would be easy on any woman who was career focused. But he knew his wife. She might balk and struggle with the idea that their lives were about to change in a drastic way, but she'd eventually accept it.

Once she accepted it, there would be no stopping her in ensuring their entire life revolved around making it work.

And yet his stomach was in knots.

"More wine?"

Brian nodded at the server while his cell phone buzzed. He glanced over at the front door but so far he was the only customer in the restaurant.

He turned over his phone that he'd laid on the table and saw a text message from Diane. *Running late. Be there soon. Order my usual, please.*

He read that again. Her usual consisted of a glass of red wine, an order of bruschetta that they would share, and the Tuscan chicken penne. He wasn't going to order her wine and he'd be shocked if she could eat the bruschetta, especially after how sensitive her stomach was last night with his garlic bread—and that was after only smelling it.

"Can I get a glass of sparkling water with lemon and an order of your Parmesan bread, light on the garlic, please." Brian waited for the server's nod before he sat back and reached for his wineglass.

"It's been a while since you were last here." A hand slapped Brian on the back and almost made him spill his wine.

"Marcello, I didn't think you were in tonight."

Brian set down his glass as the jovial Italian man sat down in the seat next to him.

"As soon as my Sara told me you were here, I came right over." He smoothed the linen and readjusted the flowers in the vase in the center of the table. "Where is that lovely wife of yours? I've missed her smile and laughter."

"She's running late."

"That woman needs to learn the art of relaxation. She needs to learn from you."

It was rare that someone would criticize Diane's work ethic, but Marcello rarely minced words.

They'd discovered Luigi's when it first opened a few years ago. From the moment they entered the restaurant, they'd felt like they'd stepped into another time and place. Marcello had transformed an old cowboy-boot factory into a rustic Italian eatery, with exposed beams, a fireplace, black-and-white photos of the "old country," and a few areas to sit comfortably on the leather sofas and chairs that ran alongside the dining area.

Diane used to say she could come in here after a long day at work and just relax. She once confessed that she'd sometimes escape during the day for a glass of wine. Marcello had created an area specifically for Diane to relax in. He'd asked for her help in creating a little sitting area, so she'd shown up one day with a leather chair and footstool, a few side tables, lamps, framed mirror, and even a small bookshelf. Every so often, Diane would bring in books and leave them there, sometimes left open, other times with a bookmark. It was her little touch, she'd say. A little touch in her little heaven.

"Her book is still on her table, you know. She hasn't come in for a few weeks now to read. I can't help but be worried."

Brian toyed with his wineglass. "Things have been a little busy for her at the office." It was killing him that he couldn't shout out to the world that they were having a baby.

"I heard about her promotion." A frown marred the large man's face as he leaned back and crossed his arms over his chest. "It's about time."

"What's with the frown then?"

"It should have happened years ago." Marcello took a wineglass offered from one of the servers who approached before waving the man off.

The front door opened and a couple walked in, hand in hand. A server approached them, offering to take their coats before leading them to a table.

"Ah, I remember when the two of you would come in like that, holding hands. You'd stare into each other's eyes, sharing your meals and dessert. You'd spend hours here, relaxed and enjoying life. Seems like a lifetime ago, doesn't it?" A speculative gleam filled Marcello's eyes as he glanced at Brian.

Sadly, it did.

"You know what you need?"

"A vacation? Trust me, I've thought about it. Now's not a good time for Diane. Maybe a weekend away, though. Any suggestions?"

"No, no, not a vacation. Although"—his brows wiggled as a smile grew across his face—"a weekend away might be perfect. My cousin owns a cabin up in the mountains if you're interested. But no, what you need, my dear friend, is a little bambino." His hands flew outward, as if he were announcing to the whole restaurant his brilliant idea.

Brian only wished he'd kept his voice down, for at that moment in walked Diane.

He studied her as she crossed the room toward him. Her shoulders were stiff and there was a frown on her face. Had she heard? God, he hoped not. That was the last thing he needed to deal with tonight.

"Diane!" Marcello rose and held out his arms.

Diane threw Brian a wary look but returned Marcello's hug.

"We were just talking about you." Marcello pulled back and took her hands in his. "You look tired. Weary. You work too hard. You don't come here enough anymore." He pouted. Brian pushed his chair back and stood.

"I'm sorry, Marcello," Diane said. "Work has been . . . difficult lately and I haven't been able to get away as often as I would like."

Brian studied his wife. Her words were stilted, her posture tight. Something was wrong.

"Come, come. Sit down and I'll get you a glass of your favorite wine." He led to her a chair beside Brian, pulled it out, and waited for her to sit.

Diane glanced down at the glass of water in front of her and shook her head. "Not tonight, Marcello. Water is good. Maybe some tea later, please?"

The bushy brows on the man's face rose before he turned and gave an overly dramatic wink to Brian. "Of course, of course. Anything for you."

Brian shook his head as Marcello walked away and couldn't stop the smile as it grew on his face.

Unfortunately, the moment he turned his attention back to Diane, that smile melted away.

"You told him?"

CHAPTER TEN

Brian sat back in alarm.

"Of course not. Why would you think that?"

Diane gave him *the* look. The one that made him feel like a fool for even asking such a stupid question. The look that had him wishing he were anywhere but here. *That* look.

"It was kind of hard not to hear him shout out the word 'bambino.'"

Brian tried to break the tension by laughing but it came out like a snort instead.

"No, no. He was telling me how you needed to slow down, enjoy life, and that a baby was the way to do it. That's all." He reached for her hand. "Promise."

Diane remained skeptical. She withdrew her hand.

"Does he honestly think a baby would slow down our lives?"

Brian shrugged. It didn't matter what he said; he wouldn't win.

"Try make it busier. I don't understand how some of the women at the office do it, juggle family and work." She sipped at her water while the server came and brought the Parmesan bread.

"Hope you don't mind. After the way you reacted to my garlic bread last night, I wasn't sure how the bruschetta would make you feel. I thought the Parmesan might be a better choice." Brian babbled, like he often did when he was uncertain.

Diane reached for a piece and smiled. "Actually, today's a good day. I'm hungry, believe it or not." She bit into the Parmesan-coated bread and sighed. "This is so good," she mumbled between bites.

The knot in Brian's stomach uncoiled while the weight on his shoulders lifted. Maybe he was worried over nothing.

"You mean you'll actually eat tonight? This calls for a celebration," Brian teased.

"Can you believe some women have morning sickness for months? I couldn't do that. I love food too much." She took another piece and devoured it. Brian reached for the last remaining slice and bit into it before Diane even noticed.

"Do you think yours is over?"

Diane nodded. "God, I hope so." She leaned forward, rested her elbows on the table, and glanced around the restaurant.

Tables were starting to fill up and the noise level rose around them. Marcello's booming voice welcomed people as he met them at their various tables while waiters scurried around the room.

"Why didn't we do this sooner?" When Diane smiled at him, there was a light in her eyes, something he'd missed seeing for a long time.

"We need to make it a priority again, don't we?" He reached for her hand again and entwined his fingers with hers. When she smiled at him, all was right in his world. It was funny how one person made that much of a difference to him.

He never believed in soul mates until Diane came into his life. He'd known the moment he caught sight of her that she was the one for him. It had been an early morning and they were the only two in a small coffee shop. He'd sat down beside her in the armchairs by the fireplace and pretended to read the morning paper, but he couldn't keep his eyes off her. Within minutes, they'd started to chat; the next thing he knew, she was asking him out on a date. They ended up having a picnic, watching the fireworks light up the sky, and the rest was history, so to speak.

Diane completed Brian in a way he never thought possible. She inspired him to be a better man, a better husband. Believed in him when no one else did. She didn't just complete him; she made him want to be someone he never thought he could be.

"It's been a while since we last went on a date. What happened to us, Brian?" Diane's voice hitched.

"Life. Work. Busy schedules. It happens." He shrugged. "Remember what the counselor told us a few years ago? That sometimes we'll have to take a backseat to life, but as long as we remember not to get too comfortable back there, that we can't always be on autopilot, we'll be fine." Brian swallowed.

He'd hated those counseling sessions. He'd thought they were fine, that their marriage was smooth sailing, until he started noticing all the marriage help books lying around the house. Apparently, Diane had other thoughts.

"Are you traveling again anytime soon?"

Brian shook his head. "No, with Marie heading up the new office in London, I'm homebound for the next little while. It'll be nice to not travel so much, to just be home." He smiled. "Who knows, I might tackle some of those projects on the honey-do list you have." He winked.

"Oh really?" He heard the skepticism in her voice.

"Or maybe find a handyman," he admitted. As much as he hated it, his skills were with computers and not with tools. The last time he'd tried to fix a leaky faucet he'd caused a slight flood in their kitchen.

He wasn't sure if now was the time to mention this, but what the heck. "What do you think about moving?"

Diane pulled her hand away from his. "Move? As in houses or cities?"

"Houses. Maybe something a bit larger, with more room."

The smile disappeared from Diane's face.

"Why? I like our condo. It suits us."

Brian took a sip of his wine. "I know. But we've been there a long time. I did some looking, and in today's housing market, we could make a pretty penny on our place and—"

Diane held up her hands. "Wait. You've been looking? For how long, and why am I only hearing about this now?" She shook her head.

"No. I don't want to move. There's no reason to, and especially not now. I don't have the time, Brian."

"You wouldn't have to do anything. I'd take care of it all, and we'd hire movers to come in." He leaned forward and almost cringed at the pleading tone to his voice. "This is the perfect time, Diane. Just think about it. Our house isn't big enough for a baby. We don't even have an extra bedroom."

Diane bit her lip. "The baby. You want the baby to have its own room. That's what this is about."

"Of course," Brian agreed. Did she only just realize that?

"Brian . . ." She sighed and took a sip of her water. "There's something we need to talk about." She stopped, glanced away from him, and leaned back, crossing her legs, as if trying to distance herself from him as much as possible.

No way. He wasn't going to allow that to happen. He'd hoped to have this conversation later, after dinner, but that idea was ruined. If they were going to talk about this, they were going to do it the right way. He moved his chair closer and forced her hand into his. She tugged for a bit, as if not wanting any contact with him, but he refused to give in.

"Diane, I know that the idea of us having a baby has turned your world upside down, but we can figure this out. Together." He needed her to hear the sincerity in his voice. He needed her to believe him.

"What if I like my world exactly as it is right now?"

Of course she did. She wasn't one for change. Unless it was planned. And this baby was anything but planned.

"Our baby will make it even better."

She gave a tight shake of her head. "Brian, what if I don't want this baby? What then?"

He rubbed his forehead. "You don't mean that. I know you don't." Didn't they just have this discussion?

"I do. I know you didn't believe me this morning when I said that, but it's true. Having a baby is the last thing I want. There's nothing inside of me that is happy about this. Nothing. I've tried, I really have." She leaned forward and started to rub his hand with her thumb. "Brian, I've thought long and hard about this and in the end, I only see one outcome that is beneficial to us both."

At that moment, their server arrived with their plates of food.

Brian pulled his hand away from Diane, not wanting to touch her. He picked up his knife and fork once their waiter left and sliced into his steamed chicken and pasta. When his knife scraped across his plate, a shiver ran along his spine. He refused to look at Diane, to see the expression on her face, to read the unspoken words in her gaze. So instead, he took a bite of his noodles and struggled to swallow.

Moments of awkward silence bound them together, neither saying a word. The only noise he heard was the clatter of their silverware against their plates. Everything else disappeared.

"Nothing scares me more right now than what might happen once this child is born. What if I can't do it? What if I can't cope? What if—"

"Stop." The nerves in his body were strung tight and he could feel his muscles bunching together. What little food he eaten settled in his stomach like a hard stone, and he knew he couldn't eat another bite. "We can't play the *what-if* game, Diane. We can't. What happened to your mother will not happen to you. It won't."

"You don't know that. Even the doctor said there was no guarantee."

Brian's jaw clenched.

"No." He breathed deeply and refused to show his anger. "No, that's not what he said. He told us that they couldn't be positive that psychosis was hereditary." He played with the napkin on his lap before folding it and laying it by his plate.

"Please tell me you haven't thought about having . . ." He couldn't finish the sentence. The word just wouldn't make it past his tongue.

Diane leaned back in her chair and crossed her arms, the rest of her food forsaken. Brian set down his fork and swallowed the food he had struggled to chew. It tasted like sawdust.

Diane said the words he didn't want to hear. "Have an abortion? Yes, actually, I have."

His world crumbled in that moment. His mind blanked, unsure of how to process something he'd never thought he'd have to deal with. Abortion. How could she?

"I'm too old, Brian. We're too old."

He shook his head. He wanted to deny her words, deny the truth of them. They weren't too old. They hadn't even hit their mid-thirties yet.

"Plus, it's too late in the game for me. If I were at the beginning of my career, maybe, but I'm not. I've worked hard to get to where I am now and I don't want to give that up."

He just blinked. He couldn't believe what she was saying. One moment it was her fear of history repeating itself and the next it was about her career. It was as if she couldn't make up her mind. He thought she'd be past all this by now, that she'd realize their child wasn't an inconvenience, that she wasn't giving up anything, but getting something that would change their lives.

"I don't want my life to change," she said.

"Don't you think you're being a little selfish here?" He blurted that out but he didn't regret it. She was being selfish. This wasn't the woman he married. Not at all. Hormones alone couldn't account for this either.

"Selfish? I'm being selfish? Who are you to say that? Are you the one who had to deal with being sick? Are you going to stay home and raise our child? Are you willing to sacrifice everything for a baby?" Her nostrils flared as she shot her words at him.

His jaw hurt from clenching it so tight.

"I would sacrifice everything. Not just for our child, but for you as well." Each word was said with measured precision.

A flash of doubt crossed her face moments before the mask he hated with every essence of his being covered her face.

Disdain. As if she were better than him. Knew more than he did.

"You say that now, but push come to shove you wouldn't," she went on. "You're a man. You have no idea what it's like to be a woman in a man's world."

"Oh, come on, Diane. It's not like you're going to get fired for having a baby."

"No. I won't get fired. Walter wouldn't do that. You're right."

He couldn't believe what he was hearing.

"Let me get this right. You're choosing your job over our baby." He cracked his knuckles and held his breath.

Diane rolled her eyes.

"Get over yourself already. I'm not choosing anything. You asked me a question and I answered. I should have known you couldn't handle the truth. You never can."

Brian's heart sank. Did she honestly see him that way?

"Abortion, though? That should be a last option, not the *only* option." Brian needed her to see his point.

She rolled her eyes at him.

"I never said it was. God, would you just listen to me for a change? What is with you?"

"I *am* listening." Brian folded his arms over his chest.

"No, no, you're not. You haven't listened to me since the moment you found out I was pregnant."

"That's not true. You know it's not. Don't turn this around on me, Dee. That's not fair."

Diane's mouth opened and then closed. Tears glistened in her eyes.

"You haven't called me that in years."

"Sure I have." He called her that all the time, didn't he?

Her lips tightened before she swiped at the tears on her face.

"You haven't called me that since we last talked about having children and I said I wasn't ready, that we needed to reevaluate our goals and timeline and think about whether having a baby was the right decision for us." All the fight left Diane at that moment. Her shoulders bowed and her head hung lower than before.

"I'm sure I have." Why was she so fixated on this? He knew he'd called her by her nickname tons of times. It was second nature to him.

"You haven't. I've noticed. It's like my not wanting a child puts a wedge between us. I know you want this baby. I know that this is something you've wanted for a long time, and I feel horrible that I don't feel the same way. Don't you think that eats away at me? What kind of woman am I not to want children?" Her lips trembled. "But then I think, *What kind of mother will I be for our child?* And deep down, I know the answer."

"Don't say that. Please don't say that. Of course you want our baby. Deep down, you know you do. You're just confused and—"

"I'm not confused." Diane cut him off. "I just want things to go back to the way they used to be."

Brian tilted his head back until he stared at the ceiling. No matter what he said, no matter what he did, it wasn't going to be enough, was it? He could argue with her until he was blue in the face. He could promise her the moon but it wouldn't matter. She couldn't see past herself.

"So what are you saying?" If she wanted him to listen, so be it. He'd listen. He couldn't promise to understand, but he'd sure as hell listen.

"I'm saying . . ." She pushed her plate away and glanced around the restaurant. "I don't know what I'm saying. It's not like I really have a choice. That's what angers me the most."

Brian leaned forward and stared his wife in the eyes. He read the conflicting messages in her face.

"You do have a choice. You've always had a choice."

Diane gave him a sad smile before she picked up her purse and looped it over her shoulder.

"I know. I can choose you, our life, and this baby. Or I can choose myself. My dreams. My goals. Me." She stood up and looked at him.

"Not much of a choice, is there?" She leaned down and placed a soft kiss on his forehead. She lingered there, and Brian felt the tears well up in his own eyes. He went to reach for her hand but she stepped back and walked away from him.

He watched her leave him. He should have stopped her or even followed after her. But he didn't. He couldn't.

He couldn't help but think she'd just made her choice, and a part inside of him died.

CHAPTER ELEVEN

Diane

Present—May

It's amazing how you can tell a day will be different than the one before the moment you wake up.

I didn't like the feel of today. There was something off. Maybe it was the way heavy dark clouds blocked the rising sun out my window or the brisk feel of the wind against my skin through its small opening.

I pulled my housecoat tight to my body and rolled a kink out of my neck while listening to Grace's tiny puffs of breath through the baby monitor.

I wanted to head back to bed and curl up in a tight ball. I could almost feel the suffocation of the heavy blankets upon me as I would drift back to sleep. But instead of doing what I wanted to do, I remained at my post by the window and waited for the sun to peek through the clouds.

If I could just see the sun, maybe the heaviness would disappear.

Last night, both Nina and Charlie managed to convince me that today I should go for a walk. I'm not sure how it happened, but I think it had something to do with Nina going on strike with her fresh-baked goods and Charlie's bribe of a mocha from the coffee shop on the other side of the park.

But, to be completely honest, it probably had to do with the plea from Charlie to get out of the house and do something together.

I haven't quite confessed my panic attacks to her yet.

———

"You can do it. Just breathe. In and out, in and out."

Nina's soft, comforting voice brought me back from whatever brink I was about to fall over. I squeezed her hand and did exactly that. Breathed in and out.

"We're going to open the door now. Let's do it together. Place your hand on the knob . . . that's it, you can do it."

I focused on Nina and her voice. Together, we managed to get my hand on the knob and with her help I was able to turn it so the door could open. But that's as far as I got before my lungs squeezed tight and I couldn't suck in any air.

Nina must have caught the panic on my face. She turned me toward her and forced me to look at her. She didn't say a word, just held on to my hands and waited for me to relax. After a moment, she started to count.

"One." She paused. "Two." Another pause. "Three." She squeezed my hand.

"Four," I whispered. By now my lungs relaxed and let in the much-needed air. My shoulders relaxed and I was able to let go of her and rub my clammy palms on my pant leg.

"I can't do this."

Since when I did take the defeatist route? I was slowly beginning to hate myself, hate the person I was becoming. But there was nothing I could do to stop it either.

Nina nodded. "You can. Let's start by just sitting outside on the porch bench. I'll grab some water."

I glanced behind me to reassure myself that Charlie was still with Grace. She was so quiet, like a little angel lying in her stroller. Charlie, on the other hand, looked like she was ready to flee at any moment. Guilt ate at me because I knew it was my fault. If only I could get my panic under control and act like a regular person about to go out on a walk with her daughter.

It's not that I didn't *want* to go for a walk. I did. I wanted to take Grace to the park and introduce her to the birds and the flowers and the laughter of the other children. I couldn't wait for the day when she was old enough to go down the slide, laugh on the teeter-totter, or learn how to pump her legs on the swing.

But what I wanted and what I could do were two completely different things.

It's as if there was a block in my head, something that stopped me from doing what I wanted to do. Or maybe it was me trying to hide myself behind a mask I wasn't sure I wanted to wear.

I knew one thing. If Brian were here, he'd be appalled at how weak I'd become. I knew Charlie was.

Make a decision already. I could hear him say. But what decision was the right one? Should I embrace the woman I was or the woman I could be?

"No." I pushed back my shoulders. "It's a beautiful day out. The walk will be good for us all."

I closed my eyes and swung the door open before I allowed myself the time to hesitate. I was going to do this. I had to do this. I didn't like who I was becoming. I didn't recognize this version of me at all.

I knew both Nina and Charlie followed me outside. Nina no doubt wore a smile on her face. Her pleasure at my insistence pushed me forward and down the stairs off my porch. I didn't worry about Grace; I knew Charlie would bring her. Other than on that first day, Charlie had refused to hold Grace again. I think she didn't want to become attached, to enjoy the feel of a baby in her arms. A stroller was safer, and while she had hesitated this morning when I asked her to push Grace, I knew she wouldn't say no.

So, I concentrated on myself, on placing one foot in front of the other. I just had to make it to the car. That was something I did on my way to work—I could do that. Once I was at my vehicle, I forced myself to take another five steps, just past the back end of the SUV, and then another five steps until I almost hit the sidewalk.

I let the warmth of the sun seep through my skin and into my bones. It felt so good. I felt so . . . free. Alive.

I lifted my face and stood mesmerized by the clouds as they drifted by. It was like I was seeing them with new eyes. What did children see when they looked at the clouds? I remembered thinking heaven sat on the clouds and that maybe if I yelled loud enough, the angels would hear me.

A smile bloomed on my face and I wanted to laugh out loud. I could do this. That was when it hit me: the realization that I hadn't succumbed to my panic attack filled me with a joy I hadn't felt in a long time. I could do this.

I turned around and beamed a smile at the women behind me. I spread my arms and laughed. Truly laughed. For once, I wasn't cold. I wasn't worried. I wasn't scared. I felt like me. The real me. The true me. The me that Brian fell in love with so many years ago, the me who loved him still.

"Well, someone seems happy." Nina smiled.

"I am." I loved hearing the laughter in my voice and I knew Nina did too.

I took hold of the stroller from Charlie, wanting to be the one to introduce Grace to the sun. Would her eyes light up at the brilliant colors? Would she hear the birds chirping above in the trees and try to see them? Would she smile at me while I picked her up and held her close?

Why had I been so afraid to bring her out?

"Should we stop at the playground on our way back?" I headed down the sidewalk.

"We could," Nina said. "I wouldn't mind sitting at the benches there and enjoying the fresh air for a bit."

Nina's cell phone rang. I watched her out of the corner of my eye as she glanced at the number and then hung back as I continued forward. I glanced over my shoulder at her but she waved me on. Who was she talking to? Was it Brian?

"Aren't you glad we did this?" Charlie asked me. I nodded but slowed my steps so I could listen to Nina's conversation.

"We're making progress. Yes . . . we're just headed on a walk. The little one is with us . . . it's a step . . . well, at this point I'll take what I can get."

I hesitated in my next step and stumbled, pushing the stroller ahead of me and out of my grip. We were at the crest of a little hill and I watched in horror as Grace rolled down the slight slope. My body froze as a scene played out in my head, of her being hit by a car as her stroller gained speed and crossed the street. A sudden jolt of pain shot through my heart before I took off running after her.

The sound of my shoes slapping against the pavement along with Nina's shouts for me to stop echoed in my ears. My arms flailed as I reached out for the stroller's handle. With a jerk, I pulled the stroller toward me just as we reached the end of the sidewalk. A pickup truck screeched to a stop just feet away, blaring his horn. I jerked back and glared at the driver. He almost hit my baby!

"It's okay, baby; Mommy's got you. Mommy's got you."

"Diane!"

With a firm grip on the stroller, I turned to find Charlie steps away from me.

"Don't. Do. That. Again." Nina sucked in a deep breath after each word.

"She was going to get run over."

"My God, Diane. You could have been hit." Charlie's body shook as she stood there. She hugged herself as she frowned at me.

"Grace almost was!" Did she not just witness that?

"How could you be so foolish?" Charlie blinked and rubbed at her eyes.

She was scared. I could see it in her eyes. She honestly feared for my life.

Nina rushed up and gripped my arm. Her eyes were wide as she stared at me.

"I'm sorry," I said. "I tripped and let go of the stroller. Oh my God, Nina. Grace could have been hit!" I placed my hand on top of hers and squeezed. "I almost lost her." My voice hitched as my throat tightened.

I almost lost her. My baby. She would have died if I hadn't caught her in time. I rushed to the front of the stroller and lifted the covering to find my daughter fast asleep.

Relief washed over me as my legs wobbled and then my knees buckled. I dropped to the ground as I stared at my sweet baby. Her lashes fluttered as her face scrunched into a frown and I realized that by my lifting the blanket, the sun now shone directly on her. I lifted my hand to block the sunlight and watched as her face relaxed. She was okay.

"She's okay. Still asleep. She never knew what happened." I smiled up at Nina.

"Of course she didn't." Charlie muttered under her breath. I caught the scowl on Nina's face as she frowned at Charlie.

What was going on between those two?

And why wasn't Charlie as relieved as I was? This was her niece. Her family. Didn't she realize how close that had been? Didn't she care? She barely glanced down at Grace. What was going on?

And what about Nina? What was up with her? She seemed more concerned for me than for Grace, and she was supposed to be the nanny.

Why did it seem like they both cared more about what happened to me than to my daughter?

———

My hand shook as I waited for the beep from Brian's answering machine.

"Damn you, Brian. Why don't you ever pick up? Why am I always leaving you voice messages? Damn it, our daughter almost died and you weren't here. Where the hell are you?"

I screamed that last bit into the phone before I chucked it across the bedroom and sank to my knees, sobbing from the anger welled up inside of me.

Where was he? What was going on with him? Did he leave me but forget to tell me? Was there an accident and he was in some hospital as a John Doe and no one knew how to reach me?

Where was my husband?

I grabbed a pillow off my bed and screamed into it. I couldn't do this anymore. Why was I suddenly so alone, forced to live a life I wasn't ready to live? I didn't want this life; it was Brian who convinced me to keep the baby, Brian who promised he would be by my side, Brian who swore I wouldn't raise this child on my own.

What good were his promises now?

If he were here, I'd hit him. Slap him so hard that the palm of my hand would sting and the sound of flesh hitting flesh would ring in both our ears. Then I'd pound my fists into his chest before throwing my arms around him and telling him how much I loved him and missed him. I hated him, loved him, missed him, and needed him too much.

Nina would say that I should focus on myself and not worry about Brian. She would say that I needed to get strong, to rebuild whatever I felt I'd lost.

I felt like I'd lost everything, though, so how could I re-create it all?

The only thing I had left was Grace. Sweet, angelic Grace who had no idea of the world she'd been born into. Her father had gone missing and her mother had gone crazy.

"Diane?"

"Go away." I stayed hunched over, sobbing into the pillow pressed tight to my face. I was tired of Nina always seeing me at my lowest.

The door creaked open.

"Leave me alone!" My throat hurt from screaming so hard. I threw the pillow toward the door, not watching to see where it landed.

The scene from earlier played over in my mind. Over and over and over.

The look on Charlie's face when I told her Grace was okay. The way she concentrated on my well-being rather than my daughter's. How she barely glanced at the stroller as we continued our walk, pretending nothing happened.

"Diane, we need to talk."

The pillow I'd thrown at the door dropped to my side. I glanced up to find Nina kneeling beside me, holding a glass of water in her hand. She held it out to me.

I tried to swallow but by now my throat was raw. I took the glass and sipped until half of the liquid inside was gone.

"What? What's there to talk about? According to you, I almost got myself killed for something as insignificant as my daughter's life." I started to laugh. What else could I do? Within a matter of minutes, I'd experienced anger, despair, and now . . . now what?

"I was scared. I handled that wrong. I'm sorry." Nina helped me stand to my feet. My legs were numb and I almost lost my balance. "Please forgive me?"

I sat down on my bed and curled my legs beneath me. Nina sat down opposite me. The silence between us stretched until I nodded.

"How are you feeling right now? Do you have a headache? Are you nauseous?"

"I feel out of control. It's like I'm on an emotional roller coaster that has no end." I leaned back on my hands and noticed Grace's bassinet on my bed. My hand shot out and grabbed hold of one of the handles. I'd almost forgotten about her.

It was like being sucker punched. I'd almost forgotten about her.

"Grace." I whispered her name, horrified at the realization.

"Shh, now. It's all right." Nina placed her hand on my knee.

I shook my head. No, it wasn't all right. It was far from all right.

"I forgot about her. I forgot about Grace. Don't tell Brian. Please, please don't tell Brian," I pleaded to Nina. "What kind of mother am I?"

Relief shone in Nina's eyes and I hated her for a brief moment. She shook her head, as if she could read my thoughts.

"No, no. It's okay. Never doubt the kind of mother you are. The moment you realized you were pregnant, you did everything you could to protect her."

I shook my head, wanting to object.

Nina stopped me.

"Trust yourself, Diane. We talked about this, remember? Yes, in the beginning you weren't sure you were ready to have a baby, but every time there was a choice between taking care of the child inside of you or doing what you wanted, like having a drink, you always chose your child over yourself. You are the perfect kind of mother. One who put her child ahead of herself. Always. It doesn't matter how long your child is with you, once a mother, always a mother."

"I need Brian. I need him here, Nina. Why isn't he returning my calls or e-mails? It's been too long, Nina. He's been gone too long." My voice hitched as I begged her to give me an answer.

"Diane—"

"No." I fisted the covers in my hand. "Don't you find that odd? I heard him ask you for updates before he left. Have you? Has he responded?"

At the widening of her eyes, it was like a light went off. I shot up from the bed and slapped Nina. Hard. My hand stung as her cheek flamed red.

"You have. And you haven't told me." Betrayal swept through me. She'd lied to me. "How could you?" My body vibrated with anger. Nina just stared up at me. She didn't say a word. Nothing to exonerate herself or explain why she'd kept silent. Nothing.

"Get out." My voice was low but steady. Despite the whirling chaos, I was centered. Calm. I knew one thing and one thing only.

"Get out of my room. Get out of my house. Stay away from me and my family."

I took a step back and watched as she slowly got to her feet. I couldn't read the look on her face. For a moment, I could have sworn she was proud of me, but then in the next moment, I could tell she was worried.

I wanted to stop her, to tell her I was sorry, that I didn't mean it, but I didn't.

I just prayed she knew. I wasn't sure what I would do without her.

CHAPTER TWELVE

Brian

May 2013

I can't believe I let you talk me into doing this."

Brian held tight to Diane's hand as he led her up the walkway to the house he knew was meant for them. He fell in love with it the moment he first saw it on the real-estate website. Now he just needed Diane to feel the same way.

It was perfect. From the white picket fence to the garden walkway and front porch where they could drink their coffee early in the morning and wave to their neighbors. The side garage didn't detract from the front of the house, and the backyard left plenty of room for a child or two to play in, maybe even a puppy.

"Just keep an open mind." Brian squeezed her hand as they followed the real-estate agent up the porch steps.

It had taken quite a bit of convincing on Brian's part to get Diane here. He'd been working on her slowly, showing her home designs and listings and throwing out ideas on what they could do in a different house for the past two months. With her morning sickness over, her mood improved and there was no more talk of not having their baby. Actually, there wasn't much talk of the baby at all.

"I'm going to let you two just walk through the house while I sit out here on the porch and enjoy the beautiful weather. Let me know if you have any questions." The Realtor stepped out of the way while Brian led Diane through the open door.

The moment he heard her tiny gasp he knew everything would be okay.

Brian wasn't even sure how to describe this house. It was home. He felt that the moment he'd first seen it and he was sure Diane felt it now. At least, he hoped she did. It was clean, simple, and bright with clear and crisp lines. It had the wide trim work around the doors and windows like Diane loved, a white bookshelf right in the entranceway, and the chocolate-colored hardwood she always raved over.

He couldn't wait for her to see the kitchen, though.

"You feel it, don't you?" He wrapped his arm around her waist and held her close as she took in all the details. He followed her gaze as she studied the circular staircase going upstairs and then looked through the French doors into a large study with a sparkling chandelier over an antique secretary desk.

Brian pointed to the back wall. "I bet the owner is a writer. Or a librarian." It would explain the many bookshelves throughout the house.

"I love the office." Diane beamed a smile at him as she opened one of the French doors and stepped into the office. Framed book covers lined one wall; on another rested an enormous corkboard where pictures and scraps of paper were pinned.

"Can't you see yourself working in here?" Make it personal. That was his goal today. To help his wife see herself in this house.

She trailed her hand down the arm of a large leather chair and sighed.

"It's gorgeous and exactly what I'd picture a writer's office to look like, if a writer did live here."

He reached for her hand and led her into the living room. He imagined them sitting there, on the couch in front of the fireplace, both with books in hand while their little one slept in a bassinet beside them. Tranquil. At peace. He pulled Diane into his arms and gave her a kiss. The look of surprise in her eyes melted away as she leaned forward and pressed herself into him, kissing him back.

"You like this house, don't you?" She placed her hand on his chest and smiled. He loved to see that, to see how easily it came. Today was a good day.

"I do. I'll tell you why after, though. I want you to see the rest."

He led her through to the kitchen. He expected a similar response to when they first walked into the house—a slight gasp—but there was nothing. She pulled her hand from his and leaned against the kitchen counter instead.

"Don't you like it?"

She shrugged.

He glanced around the room, puzzled at how she couldn't like this room. From the antique white stain to the stainless-steel appliances, it was a chef's dream come true. Or his dream, at least.

"It's a nice kitchen, Brian. Actually, it's a gorgeous kitchen. I have a feeling every room in this house is like this—well thought out, extensive detail, and everything anyone could ever want. I'm not sure what you're expecting from me. Do you want me to fall in love with it? I think you already have." She pushed herself away from the counter and grabbed one of the bottles of water left on the counter with a sign for guests to help themselves.

"I was thinking that maybe you could see yourself making this place our home." Maybe he'd been fooling himself.

The look in Diane's eye was one he'd only seen a few times during their marriage. It wasn't often that Diane took a step back and gave in, not unless she knew that in the end the results would be worth it. But he knew that if he asked it of her, if he said he really wanted them to move into this place, she'd do it. Not because she wanted to, not because she'd fallen in love with the house, but because he had.

But that wasn't what he wanted this time. He wanted her to want this too. He needed her to want this.

"Maybe this was a bad idea." He shook his head and headed toward the front hall, passing her as she stood there, watching him.

"Where are you going?" She'd reached out and placed her hand on his arm, stopping him.

"To let the Realtor know she doesn't need to wait around." He managed to keep his voice neutral, masking his disappointment.

"You might as well show me the rest of the house before you do that." Whether she intended for him to hear the sigh or not, he did. He jerked his arm away from her touch and forced himself to take a deep breath. Getting upset wasn't going to help anything, but damn, did she need to make it so obvious?

Diane wound her fingers through his and took the lead, walking through the hallway until they were back in the main foyer. They'd missed a few rooms off the kitchen, and he wanted to show her the sunroom and then the backyard, but she pulled him along until they reached the stairway.

"Remember how we used to talk about having a spiral staircase in our house? We used to dream so much in those first years." There was a wistfulness to her words. It was one of the first things he'd thought of when he walked into this house for the first time, but he hadn't been sure if she would.

"You used to boast you'd slide down the railings in the morning." Diane smiled at him while he chuckled at the memory

"I'm not sure that would be such a good idea anymore," he said.

She placed her palm on the polished wood railing and slowly climbed the stairs.

"No, you wouldn't want to teach our son bad manners, now, would you?"

Brian swallowed hard. His chest tightened at the thought.

"Son?"

Diane continued her climb but glanced over her shoulder and smiled. "Or daughter."

Diane had just had her three-month ultrasound, but they'd decided together not to find out the sex of the baby. For a moment, he'd wondered if she'd changed her mind and convinced the technician to tell her after the fact.

"What would you like to show me first?" She stood at the top of the stairs and looked down the hallway. To the right was the master bedroom and to the left were the other rooms.

"Turn right."

When he'd first walked through the house, he couldn't believe the master bedroom. The Realtor had called it the *master wing* and hadn't lied. Half of the upstairs was dedicated to it. From the moment you walked into the bedroom it felt like another section of the house. To the left was a small sitting area, complete with electric fireplace, love seat, and a wall-mounted television, and to the right was an office section with filled bookshelves and a writing desk. Straight ahead was the bedroom; beyond that was the en suite bath.

Diane stood at the windows, curtain pulled, and glanced out into the backyard.

"What do you think?"

"It's gorgeous. I can't think of any other word to describe this house. A home most women would love to have." She turned. "This room is a haven. I'm not sure I'd want to leave. You might have to bring me my coffee and meals." She smiled at him.

"I could do that." He knew she'd been teasing, but he wasn't.

"What about you, though? Where is your dream come true? You didn't pick this house out just for me."

He cocked his head. She still didn't get it, after all these years. She didn't understand.

"You are my dream come true, Diane. You and this miracle of ours." He placed his hand gently over the tiny swell that was starting to form.

She sighed, covered his hand with hers, and placed a kiss on his lips.

"You're too good to me," she whispered into his mouth before pulling away. "What else is there to see?"

Brian smiled. "Follow me." He couldn't wait to show her one of his favorite rooms in the house. Yes, the kitchen forced his culinary cravings to run at full tilt, but it was the one room down the hall that made his heart sing the most.

"Is there a secret room full of computers and plasma screens on all the walls?" Diane laughed as she followed him out of the master bedroom and down the hall.

Brian bypassed the bathroom and the two bedrooms. There was nothing special about them. But he stopped at the only room that had a closed door. At one time, the house had had a bonus room, but the owners had torn down the wall between that room and this bedroom and created an oasis for a small child.

He waited till Diane stood beside him and then he opened the door.

———

He would never forget the first time he saw this room.

The walls were cream and on one hung a carpet that Brian knew would be soft to the touch. A crib painted antique white sat in front of that wall with a blanket the color of sand draped over it. The room spoke of elegance, and he knew right away that Diane would love it. In one corner sat a rocking chair; in another was a large unique wooden rocking horse.

"It's beautiful." Diane squeezed his hand before heading toward the horse and trailing her fingers over its thick mane.

"It's perfect, isn't it?" Brian couldn't contain the joy in his voice. She liked it. A small part of him had been worried, unsure if this was the type of room she'd want for their baby. He would have preferred a more regular baby room, with some blue or pink, but he knew that might be going too far for Diane.

She stopped in front of the crib, one hand on the blanket while she touched the carpet on the wall.

"I've seen this look in magazines before. It's nice. I like how it softens the room." She turned, leaning on the crib, and rubbed her belly.

Brian stepped closer to her and covered her hand with his. "I thought it might be the perfect room for our little one."

Diane's eyes relaxed at his words and a shot of pure joy swept through him. His goal was to have her as excited about their baby as he was. She wasn't there yet, but she would be.

"I'm surprised. I thought you would want to go all out and paint the room pink or blue and I'd have to convince you to accent in color instead." There was a twinkle in her eye. "But I can see why this is your favorite room. I can picture you at night, in the rocking chair, trying to get your son or daughter to sleep." The edges of her lips teased into a smile as she wrapped her arms around him and leaned close. "I hope the room is soundproof so at least one of us can sleep."

Brian pulled back. "Who said I get all the night watches?"

"I was thinking more along the lines of you teaching our child code in the middle of the night. It always works to put me to sleep." She shrugged while playfully flicking at his chest with her finger. He caught her hand, brought it up to his lips, and laid a kiss on her palm.

"Seriously, I think this house, this room, is perfect for us. Don't you?" Brian asked.

He watched the rise in Diane's chest, the way she arched her back and then turned from him to study the room.

"It does give us more room to grow in . . ." Her voice tapered off.

"But?" He wasn't sure he liked where this was going.

Diane sighed. "No buts. I like it. It's perfect. There are just so many changes coming at once. I like our condo and our condo living."

The tight band that had been squeezing his heart loosened. He could hear in her voice that she was scared. Too much change in her personal life rattled her. It always did. He should have been more aware of it.

"What if you let me take care of this? You concentrate on work and everything you need to do before our baby arrives and I'll handle everything else." If he could take out all the negatives, maybe she'd give in and realize moving would be good for them.

"You're going to handle moving? Packing, cleaning, unpacking, setting things up, painting, repairing . . . getting our place ready for listing? You're going to take care of all that?"

He nodded. "How hard can it be? I'll hire a moving company, and we'll get the cleaners to come in a couple of extra times."

Diane chuckled. "Just like a man to get others to do the work. I know it's been a few years, Brian, but there's more to it than just hiring a cleaning company and movers."

Brian shrugged. He'd figure it out. "If I take care of it all, will you think about it?"

Her lips pursed. "Brian—"

He shook his head. "No." He stopped her. "Just think about it, okay?"

She tilted her head and gazed around the baby's room again.

"Okay."

Brian tried very hard to keep the smile off his face as he reached for her hand and they walked out of the room and back down the stairs.

All she needed was some time. Eventually she'd come around and see that they needed to move and that this house was more than perfect for them. He'd keep the pressure down, only mention it in passing, and see if she came to the decision herself.

No pressure. That would be his motto for the next few months.

At the bottom of the stairs, the Realtor stood waiting for them. She held a clipboard full of paper with a pen attached to the top.

"So, how was the tour? I'm sure you fell in love just as hard as Brian did all the other times we walked through. I have all the paperwork here and just need your signature, Diane, to finalize everything." She held the clipboard out.

Diane crossed her arms and turned toward Brian. "Finalize? You signed already?"

Brian cringed when he caught the deadly look in her eyes. Didn't matter that she kept a smile on her face. He knew he was in trouble just from the way one finger tapped her arm.

The Realtor took a step backward and withdrew the clipboard, only to have Diane take it from her.

"I'm so sorry. I thought . . . Why don't I give you both a few minutes to talk this over?" The Realtor's face flushed as she stepped back out onto the porch.

An uncomfortable silence filled the hallway as Brian watched Diane read through the papers.

"I knew you didn't have time to do a lot of house shopping—"

"So you went ahead and did it without me." Diane's voice was low as she flipped through the pages.

He cleared his throat. "I only looked at a few places." Brian shrugged.

"You didn't think about talking to me first? I thought we were a team."

Brian wasn't sure how to respond to that. They were a team, but lately he felt like he was the only one planning for their future as a family.

"Before I mentioned it, did you have any thoughts that maybe the condo would be too small for all of us?"

Diane shook her head.

"And that's why we make such a great team. You don't have to think about this stuff because you know I will. Who was the one who found our condo?" Brian stepped forward and wrapped his arms around his wife, whose lips lifted in a smile.

"You," she said.

"Exactly. If I hadn't, we might still be living in that one-bedroom apartment with Mrs. Higgins, the crazy cat woman, across the hall from us."

When Diane laughed, the tension around Brian's heart eased.

"I almost forgot about her." She wrinkled her nose. "Do you remember that awful fish smell?"

Brian nodded. "The one that greeted you the moment you stepped off the elevator? Yeah, I'll never forget it."

They both stood there with silly grins on their faces at the memory. Brian knew he would always remember this time between them.

"You know"—Diane turned in his arms so that her back was against his chest—"I think the house is perfect. Let's take the papers home with us so I can look them over and then we can set up a coffee time with the Realtor so we can sign them together. How does that sound?

Brian stood there, arms around his wife, and grinned. Did she just say what he thought she said?

"Are you sure?" This had to be a joke. No way she would have decided this quickly. Not Diane. She needed time to process it, to weigh the pros and cons. Time for him to talk her into it. This wasn't the woman he married.

"Absolutely." She turned, gave him a quick kiss on the lips, and then stepped out of his arms and pushed open the screen door.

Brian's world went a little off-kilter. He had expected a battle of wills and that he'd need time to convince her that this was the right move. Not in a million years had he expected her to agree just like that.

Maybe that's what the problem was. He expected her to fight him when he should have been prepared for her to fall in love with the place as much as he did.

"Wonderful!" The Realtor's voice boomed as he followed Diane out to the front porch. "I have an opening later this evening, if that works. I can come and take a look at your place at the same time," she said before she left them on the porch.

Brian reached for Diane's hand and walked with her to their car. He glanced back over his shoulder and only one word came to mind as he looked on the house.

Home.

CHAPTER THIRTEEN

Diane

Present–May

A re you sure this is such a good idea?"

We sat in my vehicle, Charlie at the wheel because she hates being a passenger, both of us focused on the front door to my office building. Charlie's fingers drummed on the steering wheel as she looked at me.

"Why wouldn't it be? We'll be in and out before you know it."

"Yeah, right. I know you, Diane. It doesn't take you long to get lost in your e-mails or memos or an urgent message from Walter about something." She rolled her eyes before she grabbed her purse from the back and opened her door.

I didn't bother to argue. She was right. The old me would have, but work wasn't as important to me lately. Sure, I kept tabs on things and talked to Walter on a continual basis, but today was about Charlie and spending time with her. I just needed to make a quick stop to pick up something from my office first.

"Why are we here again?"

"To pick up my notes for tonight and my dress that Amanda had dry-cleaned."

"And this is for . . . ?"

"The fund-raiser. The one I'm trying to talk you into going to . . ." I winked.

"Riiight. The one I keep saying I don't want to go to?" Her nose wrinkled, something she used to do as a child when I forced her into a situation she didn't want to be in.

I led her through the doors and down the hallway to where our offices were located on the main floor.

"Oh, come on, it'll be fun. Normally I wouldn't go, but it's for the food bank and I'm on their board. It's basically one of the only parties I can't miss. Besides, when I RSVP'd I added a plus one."

"You do realize I don't have anything to wear, right? Nor do I have any shoes, and I can promise you I'm not in the mood to get my hair done or pretend I'm even remotely interested in meeting anyone there." She plopped down in one of the chairs opposite my desk while I sat down and went to turn on my computer.

"Uh-uh. No e-mails, no messages." She wagged her finger at me. "Just find your notes, grab your dress, and we're out of here."

I rummaged through the stack of papers on my desk to find the notes I'd jotted down the last time I'd popped into the office. I knew they had to be in here somewhere. I grabbed the pile closest to me and sat down in my chair. I massaged my temple for a few seconds before glancing down at the sheets.

"Are you okay?" Charlie asked.

I looked up and squinted. Large black circles in my vision blocked out most of her face.

"Diane?" Charlie rose from her chair.

I blinked and the black circles faded. I blinked a few more times until they disappeared. This happened a few days ago too, just before I got hit with a massive migraine.

"It's just a headache."

Charlie gently massaged the sides of my head and I groaned. It felt so good. Brian used to do that for me too. A hard loneliness hit my heart at the thought. It hurt too much to think about him. I didn't understand the silence, why he ignored my texts and phone calls. Why he spoke to Nina but not me.

"Do you have any aspirin?" Charlie asked.

"In my purse."

I listened to Charlie rifle through my purse. "These?"

I opened my eyes to see an orange prescription bottle in her hand.

"No, it's an actual aspirin bottle. I don't know what those are." I reached for them and read the label, hoping for it to tell me what they were. But the only information on the bottle was my name and then how many pills to take and how many times a day.

Was this a new prescription? It couldn't be. I didn't remember placing these in my purse, let alone getting them filled or even seeing a doctor. I opened the cap and let some of the pills fall into my hand. These weren't the regular white pills I took at night during tea with Nina. These pills were pink and yellow and circular.

Charlie must have caught my hesitation as I placed them down on my desk. She grabbed the phone and called Nina.

"Diane has a headache." She rubbed my shoulder while she listened to Nina.

"Right, I found those. Are those . . . okay, how many?"

I grabbed the phone out of her hand. "What are these pills for? I don't remember them."

Nina sighed into the phone. "Your headaches. We discussed this already, Diane." There was a soft cry in the background.

"Is that Grace? And I don't remember these pills. I'm not comfortable taking more medication." The crying got louder for a brief moment before I heard the sound of a door closing and then silence.

"These are stronger and will work better with the other medication you're on. You need to take them every four hours with food. I gave you some crackers as well. Did you find those?"

"Are there crackers in there too?" I covered the mouthpiece with my hand as Charlie searched in my purse and pulled out the packs of saltine crackers Nina mentioned.

"Found them," I told her.

"Take those and we can talk when you get home about your headaches."

I opened the pack of crackers and nibbled on one as I eyed the tiny pills. I didn't want to take them. But at the same time, I wasn't sure how I would get through my meeting and the dinner tonight if I got slammed with another headache. Despite my hesitation, I popped the pills in my mouth, took a sip of water, and wished for the best. And then I made a note to talk to Nina about all these medications I seemed to be taking lately.

How could she be prescribing medication for me when I hadn't even seen a doctor?

———

"Well, look who's here! My two favorite girls."

Walter's loud voice boomed in against the walls of my office as he walked in with his arms wide open. I wasn't surprised to see him. I knew the receptionist at the front desk would have told him I'd arrived.

I cringed as his voice ricocheted in my head while Charlie almost ran into his arms. She loved Walter probably as much as I did. Walter had stepped into our lives while we lived with Aunt Mags. I never figured out how the two knew each other, but Walter would often show up at the house with bags of groceries or toys for us in those early years. We started to call him Uncle Walter shortly after that. He always seemed to be there for us whenever we needed him.

"It's so good to see you!" Walter held Charlie by the arms and looked her over. I wonder if he'd see what I saw when she first arrived. Walter normally caught the little things when it came to Charlie, the things she tried to hide from others.

"What's wrong?" His eyes narrowed as he stared at her. I caught the tiny shake of her head before he pulled her in close and wrapped her in his arms.

My relationship with Walter was different from Charlie's. Mine had evolved throughout the years as I worked alongside him. But Walter was Charlie's pseudo father. Even though I couldn't see her reaction, I knew she was struggling not to cry.

"It's going to be okay. You know that, right? Just one day at a time, there, kiddo. We'll get through this."

I leaned forward, elbows on my desk as I watched the two in front of me. What did he mean by that? Had Charlie talked with Walter about Marcus and the whole baby issue without telling me? For some reason, the thought of being left out like that really bothered me.

"It's harder than I thought it would be." Charlie pulled back but kept her hand on his arm. "Diane just needed to pop in for some notes and her dress for tonight."

Walter turned to face me.

I didn't like the attitude he was giving off. His arms were crossed over his massive chest while he directed a fierce frown my way.

"What?" I asked.

I massaged a small part on the side of my head to help with the headache.

"Why are you here? I thought I told you to take more time off." He walked closer to my desk and glared at me.

I shrugged. I wasn't in the mood to get my hand slapped. I was a grown woman. I should be the one who decided what I did or didn't do.

"I've been trying to talk her out of it all day, but she won't listen to me." Charlie sank down in a chair and refused to look at me.

"I'm not a child, so stop treating me like one, both of you." I pinched my lips together as I could feel my muscles tighten in response to the anger building up inside of me.

"No one is treating you like a child." Charlie sighed.

Really? She was really going to go there?

"You haven't let me out of your sight since the day you arrived. You follow me around the house and treat me as if I'm a china doll that will break into pieces if you say the wrong thing. Seriously, I've had enough." I sat back in my chair and crossed my own arms.

"Diane—" Walter leaned down, placing his hands on my desk, but I interrupted anything he was about to say.

"No. Walter. Don't. I've had a child. I didn't suffer a major catastrophe. I'm not an invalid." Well, other than the piercing headache . . .

"You don't look well. I'm just concerned."

"So concerned that you can't even take the time to come by the house?"

I glanced up at him and saw the concern in his eyes. I felt bad for berating him a moment ago.

"She's been getting some bad migraines," Charlie offered.

"You have one now, don't you?" Walter's gaze scrutinized me.

There was no reason to deny it—Charlie wouldn't let me anyway—so I nodded.

"You don't need to come tonight. I told you that. The board already knows you won't be there; they're not expecting you."

I rolled my eyes. He wasn't telling me anything I didn't already know. We'd discussed this over and over and over. And again this morning.

"I want to be there. There's no reason for me to miss it tonight. None."

"There's every reason!" Walter flung up his hands and paced my office.

I felt like I was in the twilight zone, where everyone was speaking a language only I couldn't understand.

"Name one," I challenged him. I glanced at Charlie for support but that was a mistake. I knew right away she wasn't going to back me in this. She was rubbing lotion on her hands and wouldn't even look me in the eye.

"Diane . . ." Walter sighed but didn't finish.

"Look, I'll stay low-key, arrive late, and leave early."

When all Walter did was shake his head, I knew he wasn't going to continue to argue with me, which was good. Maybe the issue wasn't that they were treating me like a child, but that I was letting them.

"I'm worried that you're not ready, that it will be too much all at once." Walter sat down in the chair beside Charlie and crossed his legs.

"How is this too much? Would you be this worried about me if this was before Grace's birth?"

His eyes widened at that. "Of course not."

"Then what's the issue?" I shrugged. "Besides, Charlie will be with me. It's not like I'm coming alone."

Walter turned to Charlie, who nodded.

"You promise not to overdo it?"

"Scout's honor." I held up my hand.

"Like I'm going to trust that. You weren't even in the Scouts." Walter scoffed as he adjusted his tie. "Look"—he fiddled around in the chair—"you don't need my approval, I know that. But I'm just . . . I want to take care of you, to make sure you're okay. This isn't the Diane I know and love."

That caught me by surprise.

"I'm the same woman I've always been, Walter. Why would you say that?"

"He just means you've softened since Grace. Don't you?" Charlie rushed in while Walter struggled to respond.

"Softened?" What did she mean by that? Did she mean it in a bad or good way? Was she talking about my paranoia to take Grace outside? She wouldn't hold that against me, would she?

All of a sudden, the thoughts in my mind compounded on one another until I didn't recognize them other than the awful symphony of pain that came with their whispered words. My eyes twitched as I glanced from Walter to Charlie and back to Walter. The way they were looking at each other . . . something was going on and it had to do with me. Their mouths were moving, but I couldn't hear the words they said to each other. There was a loud ringing in my ears and the black dots were coming back in my vision.

The room spun around me until I was sure I swayed in circles. I saw both Charlie and Walter rush toward me, their hands out-stretched, but then the black dots swallowed them whole as I screamed.

CHAPTER FOURTEEN

Brian

July 2013

T rust me."

Anticipation knotted in Brian's stomach as he covered his wife's eyes with a black cloth. He wanted tonight to be a night she'd always remember.

"I trust you." She smiled before twirling around so he could tie the cloth.

He led her out of their condo and to the limo that awaited them in the driveway. He helped her climb in and, after making sure they were both comfy, he tapped on the glass partition, a signal for the driver to take them away.

"Are we"—her hands caressed the black leather seats, felt along the door and then discovered the side bar to her left—"in a limo?" There was a hint of excitement in her voice and Brian loved it.

He was thrilled to be able to surprise her like this. He knew he'd caught her completely off guard.

It was their thirteenth wedding anniversary. Brian had lied earlier in the week to Diane, telling her he had to work late each night, so they'd made plans to celebrate on the weekend. Diane had bought tickets to the latest play and Brian had made reservations at a high-end steak house nearby.

So, when Diane came home to find a rose petal trail to their room, where a hot bath awaited her and a new dress, shoes, and lingerie were laid out on their bed . . . needless to say, she'd been speechless.

Next year, they'd be celebrating their anniversary with a six- or seven-month-old baby, so this year, Brian wanted to make this an extra-special memory.

"Where are we going?"

Brian reached for two glasses that had been previously poured and placed one in Diane's hand. He would have preferred champagne, but they'd have to make do with nonalcoholic juice instead.

"Here's to a night full of love, surprises, and happily ever afters." He clinked his wine flute with hers. "Here's to us."

"To us," Diane echoed.

They sipped their drinks in silence but Brian refused to release Diane's hand. He couldn't wait for her reaction when they arrived at their destination. It had taken some favors being called in to make this night happen, but it would all be worth it.

"How long have you been planning this?" Diane laid her head down his shoulder and sighed.

He knew the day had been long and tiring for her. He'd kept in touch with her by text as she ran from one meeting to another. At four o'clock, she'd texted that she needed to run across town to settle a dispute with one of their accounts, and that it required a personal touch. He'd been worried she wouldn't make it home in time.

He checked his watch. They should arrive in five minutes, plenty of time to spare.

"Long enough to be worried when you had that errand to run at the last minute today."

She chuckled. "I thought you'd be working late."

"True." He drew circles on her hand as he admired the shape of her long, muscular legs.

"I can't believe you kept this from me. What if I had been late?"

"Well, then I guess it would have been lesson learned." Brian laughed, but in reality he had been sweating bullets until she made it home.

"Do I get any clues?" She bumped her leg against his. He placed his hand on her knee, enjoyed the feel of bare skin beneath his hand, and was tempted to slide his hand up beneath her dress, but contained himself. Tonight was about building up to the moment. Almost like when they'd first met.

"You get three guesses."

"Will you tell me if I'm right?"

Brian shook his head and then remembered she couldn't see him.

"Highly unlikely. But . . . you might be surprised," he teased.

He loved to surprise her, to see her reaction, how it always caught her off guard. He loved that he could still do that after all these years.

Her cheeks were flushed, her lips curved into a smile, and if he were to remove the blindfold, he knew her eyes would sparkle. She was the most beautiful woman he'd ever met and to this day, he couldn't believe she was his.

"Are we going to Luigi's?"

"Really? You're going to waste a guess on that? This is a special night. Unless, of course, I convinced Luigi to close the restaurant for the night . . ." He managed to put enough truth in his tone to make it believable.

She gasped.

"But of course I wouldn't do that. His place is packed each night. Do you know how expensive that would be?"

He enjoyed the way she nibbled at her lip when she thought about her next guess.

"We're going out of town for the night?"

He tsked before she slapped him on the arm and laughed.

"But then you'd need to pack an overnight bag for me, and we both know that wouldn't have happened."

The vehicle slowed to a stop.

"Are we here?" Diane leaned forward as the passenger door opened.

"No peeking, remember?" Brian covered the cloth over her eyes with his hand as he backed up, opened the door, and drew her with him.

He helped her over the curb and looked around him. Excitement built up inside of him and he almost blurted out the surprise.

"Brian, where are we?" She reached up to remove the cloth but he stopped her.

"Not yet. You don't want to ruin it."

He led her through the front doors of the hotel and through the foyer. He'd stopped in earlier to ensure everything had been taken care of and he recognized the concierge. The man tipped his hat and smiled. Brian smiled back. He couldn't believe they were doing this.

With their hands entwined and Diane close to his side, he walked her though the five-star restaurant. He held his finger up to his lips and the hostesses there to greet them all smiled but kept quiet.

There was a low murmur as Brian followed one of the hostesses through the dining area. He made sure to walk slowly, as Diane still couldn't see her way and he didn't want her to bump into anyone. The restaurant was packed. Rumor had it that there was a six-month waiting list.

"Brian?"

They stopped at the doors that led into the kitchen area. He still couldn't believe he'd managed to snag something like this. Diane was going to love it. He glanced back at the people watching him from their tables. Fine china, soft cream-and-black décor, candlelight, and white roses on each table.

As beautiful as it was out there, nothing would compare to what they were about to experience.

———

"Are you ready?"

He pushed open the doors and led Diane through. Her grip on his hand tightened as the sounds of a busy kitchen surrounded them.

"Brian?"

He couldn't keep the smile off his face.

He led her over to a table located just off to the side and turned her around so her back was to him. He leaned forward, placed a soft kiss on her cheek, and whispered, "I love you" in her ear before he untied the cloth.

"Oh . . ."

Brian wound his arm around her waist and held her close as she realized where they were.

"Jean Pierre's," Diane whispered as the famous Michelin Star chef left his station and headed toward them, a large smile on his face.

"Brian!" JP shook his hand before he pulled Diane in for a hug.

"How? What?" She turned, eyes wide as she struggled to form words.

JP laughed before he slapped Brian on the back. Brian stumbled forward as he shot the chef a narrow glance. JP only shrugged.

"I hear it's your anniversary. It's not often I open my kitchen to guests, but for Brian here, I'd do just about anything."

JP was a former client of Harper and Wainright. Brian had worked with him on the side last year on a special project. It wasn't until last week that he remembered a favor was owed.

"I can't believe you did this." Diane turned, wound her arms around Brian, and smiled up at him.

Right then and there, Brian knew this was a night they would always remember.

"Anything for you," Brian whispered against her lips. She felt so good in his arms like this.

"All right, you two lovebirds. Save that for later."

A waiter pulled out Diane's chair while Brian seated himself. While their water was being poured, Diane leaned forward, elbows on the table, and listened to JP rattle off the night's menu. Brian didn't hear a single word. All he saw was the way the light reflected off Diane's hair and the shine of her skin. She glowed.

He reached for her hand and brought it down under the table, their fingers entwined. He felt like a lovesick puppy right now, and nothing could ruin that.

"How did you land this?" Diane leaned close once JP left. She ran her fingers along his thigh in teasing circles.

"I have my ways." Brian smiled.

"How do you know him? I tried to get reservations here a few years ago but they were booked for months."

"I did a favor for him last year." He smiled.

"Oh, what kind of favor?" There was a twinkle in her eye.

"One that involved removing some unwanted photos he'd mistakenly uploaded to his website," Brian leaned forward to whisper in her ear.

She gasped. He nodded. They laughed. Just like they used to when they were first married.

They couldn't stop touching each other, whether it was a caress beneath the table, the tip of a finger trailing down an arm, or a light brush against the neck. Brian couldn't get enough of his wife tonight and she seemed to be as swept up as he was.

"We really should be focusing on the chef," Diane teased as she squeezed his knee.

Brian caught JP's wink.

"I think he's enjoying the show," Diane whispered.

"I noticed that." Brian frowned at the guy. "I think he's delaying our food on purpose."

"He'd better not be. I'm quite hungry." Diane sat back in the chair and crossed her arms over her chest. She beckoned JP over with her finger.

"You summoned me?" There was laughter in his voice, thank God. This was the first private chef's meal they'd ever had, so Brian wasn't sure what to expect. He certainly didn't expect the table set up as if they were out in the main dining area, complete with crystal wineglasses, fine china, and the table arrangement. For some reason, he'd thought they'd be given a regular table with a plain tablecloth. When he'd asked the hostess earlier to see if the table could be done up nicely, he now understood the look of surprise on her face.

"Any word on our meal? I'm quite famished tonight. I'm eating for two." She lightly rubbed her belly and smiled at Brian.

JP's brows rose at this.

"I had no idea, Brian, old man. Why didn't you tell me?" JP rounded the table and kissed Diane on the cheek.

Brian bristled at the familiarity.

"Tonight is to celebrate us." Diane placed a kiss on Brian's cheek.

"Well, then, let's get this celebration started." JP snapped his fingers and waiters surrounded them with platters in hand.

Diane's eyes grew round at the sight of all the food, while Brian's stomach rumbled.

"Sure hope you're hungry." More plates were brought over, and Brian could have sworn there was enough food for everyone in the kitchen to share. He knew they were to get samplers of all the dishes, but he thought they would be just that . . . samples. Not full dishes.

Diane speared a shrimp smothered in butter and raised it to her lips. "Just don't eat too much. I have my own thoughts on dessert."

Brian was in heaven.

CHAPTER FIFTEEN

Brian

August 2013

I still can't believe you did it."

Brian raised his wineglass and clinked it against Diane's sparkling water–filled glass. They sat at their favorite table in Luigi's, celebrating the new change in their lives.

In two short months, Brian had managed to list, sell, and move them out of the condo and into the new house. He didn't want to waste any precious time getting their new home ready for their expanding family.

"*We* did it," he corrected her. Sure, he did most of the heavy lifting, organizing the moving company, the cleaning crew, and setting up their new addresses with the local companies, but if she hadn't given him a list of all the things that needed to be done, he would have failed miserably.

Diane smiled. "I'm just glad it's over."

"Diane! You're here!" Marcello's loud voice boomed throughout the restaurant. A large smile filled his wife's face and Brian just shook his head at the noisy Italian.

"Is today the day? Is that why you are here? I'm honored you would celebrate your new home with me." Marcello leaned down and placed a kiss on each of Diane's rosy cheeks. She beamed at him before nodding toward Brian.

"And you, you did it all! My son, he worked out okay, right? I told him if he messed up any of your furniture I'd send him back to the old country, where he'd learn what hard work was all about."

At Marcello's insistence, Brian had hired his son and some friends to set up the furniture in their new home and help him get things ready.

"They were fine. You should be proud." Brian patted Marcello on the back. "He's a very hard worker."

Marcello nodded. "Good. Good. You never know with kids. You can train them all you want, but when they grow old enough, you just gotta hope and pray they heard you through all the noise."

"You'll have to come over to see our new place, Marcello, and bring your lovely wife as well once we're all unpacked," Diane said.

Brian sat back, slightly amazed. She'd never invited Marcello over. In fact, the first and only time Brian had ever suggested such a thing, Diane had shot him down, saying that confining their relationship to the restaurant was all they needed.

"Really? We would love that. What an honor! I'll bring some of my best wine, the stuff I keep hidden away for only special occasions. Thank you." Marcello kissed the top of Diane's hand.

Brian watched the scene play out in front of him. It was interesting to watch his wife blush like a schoolgirl.

"What was that about?" Brian leaned forward and spoke softly as Marcello greeted guests as they walked in.

Diane shrugged.

No way, he wasn't going to let her get away with that.

"Spill. I know there must be a reason for the sudden change of heart."

Diane played with the cloth napkin on her lap, her eyes downcast in a rare moment of insecurity. Either she was playing him or this was all hormonal. Again.

"Our new place has a different feel to it. More welcoming. Friendlier. I thought maybe it was time to be the same way. More personable."

"You are. Everyone loves you."

She shook her head, disagreeing with him.

"Diane." Brian leaned forward and reached for her hand. "Honey, you're perfect just the way you are. You don't need to change."

"You have to say that. But we both know it's not true. In the past, maybe." She glanced up at him. "But lately, it seems like I've been so focused on my career that I've forgotten there's more to life."

Brian didn't know what to say. He couldn't really deny it, because she had been more focused on work than anything else. Look at how she'd acted when she first realized she was pregnant with their baby. But slowly he'd started to notice a change in her toward their baby. More accepting and . . . dare he say it . . . excited?

"Is there anything I can do to help?" He took the easy way out and didn't outright agree with her.

She chuckled. "You can agree with me, you know. I'm not going to bite your head off."

"Not now, maybe, but later you might." He leaned back in his chair and reached for a piece of the warm buttered garlic bread Marcello had brought to their table.

She winced. "Have I been that bad?"

Brian rubbed his chin and smiled. "Only if you consider throwing a pickle at my back because you thought I was ignoring you bad."

Diane covered her mouth with her napkin and started to laugh. "I'm so sorry." Her laughter was contagious and had Brian chuckling himself.

"You have to admit, though, I had a good point." Diane managed to calm her laughter but the smile remained.

Brian nodded. "Sure, but what about when you got upset over how I wrote in pen on the boxes instead of using those notecards you wanted me to use?"

She bought him over one hundred pale pink notecards and said it would make her life easier if he labeled each box with its contents on these cards, then taped them to the boxes. He'd told her she was crazy and used a black pen to mark which room the boxes should go to. Diane had thrown her hands up in frustration and actually stormed out of the house, only to return twenty minutes later with two ice-cream sundaes. Apparently, that was her way of apologizing.

He still refused to use the notecards.

"No way. Trust me, as you start looking for things, you'll be wishing you had used my idea."

In this moment of smiles and comfortable silence, Brian realized he was happy. Really happy. He couldn't wait to eat a delicious dinner and then take his wife home and make love to her for the first time in their new home.

"I think we should skip dessert tonight," Brian suggested as he took a sip of his wine.

"Really? Did you not hear Marcello tell us about the cheesecake?"

"We could take it home and eat it later." He shrugged. He could think of a few ways they could enjoy the dessert.

"Brian . . ." The tone of her voice and the way she leaned toward him gave him all the incentive he needed to make sure their dinner was enjoyable but fast. Thank God the waiter arrived with their orders. He didn't even bother to say thank-you; just grabbed his knife and started to cut his steak. This would be the fastest dinner they'd ever eaten at Luigi's.

It might only have been a week since the last time he made love to his wife, but he could have sworn it felt like a year.

"Whoa, slow down there. I'm not going anywhere anytime soon. All we have waiting for us are boxes to unpack." She shook her head. "Wait, let me rephrase that. All you have waiting for you back at the house are boxes to unpack. I plan on becoming familiar with my new bathtub before anything else happens."

Brian groaned.

"You can always dry me off," Diane suggested. She winked at him from across the table before spearing a piece of chicken from her pasta bowl.

"Besides," she said, between mouthfuls, "you'll need to find the box with our bedsheets first."

Brian growled.

"Actually, do you think we could stop by the office on our way home?"

"Diane." Now she was going too far.

"No." She shook her head. "I'm serious. There's a file I'd like you to look at when you have the time. Walter has a new idea on some program he thinks would help some of our processes, but before I hand it over to Neil I'd like you to take a look at it and see if it's even possible."

"If this is your idea of foreplay . . ." He reached for his wine to clear his thoughts. Whenever she asked him to look over one of Walter's big ideas, it usually ended up with him needing a stiff drink. This didn't bode well for him.

"You can always look it over tomorrow. We have the whole weekend ahead of us." She sat back and allowed the waiter to take her now-empty plate. Brian glanced down at his own and realized he'd hardly touched his steak or pasta.

"Right," he mumbled. "A weekend spent unpacking and trying to find a way of making Walter's dumb-ass idea into a good one. Sounds like fun." He kept his focus downward, knowing Diane probably didn't hear him, since she ordered dessert while he was speaking.

"What did you say?"

Brian sighed as he chewed on the dinner that no longer appealed to him.

"Nothing. If it makes your life easier at work, then there's nothing I'd like to do more than help you with this project."

———

The echo of Brian's cell phone as it vibrated on one of the plethora of boxes in the room had him wanting to punch something. He'd set the phone down and since then it had gone off repeatedly for the past three hours. At first he tried to ignore it. It was Saturday and the entire office knew he was off-line thanks to this move. But its incessant buzzing had gone beyond irritating.

At the time, saving money by unpacking himself seemed like a smart idea. He now realized that a more brilliant idea would have been paying for the complete package.

He'd thought Diane had been kidding when she said she wasn't unpacking. Apparently, he'd been wrong. She had no problem going out for a spa day with her girlfriends while he slaved away trying to find items in boxes that he should have labeled better.

Damn Diane and her notecards. Damn his pride in thinking he could do it better.

What he needed was a nice cold beer, but that meant stopping so he could drive to the liquor store, and he wanted to get as much put away as possible. At least the movers had placed boxes in the right rooms. He'd leave Diane's office boxes for her to unpack on her own and his own office boxes for later. But the kitchen, bathrooms, bedrooms, and countless knickknacks and clothes—it was all too much.

He wouldn't admit defeat, though. Maybe he'd call Marcello's son and see if he wanted to make some extra money. Perhaps if the kid had a girlfriend, he'd even bring her along. Heck, he'd be willing to pay her double just to get the kitchen started for him. In this case, he had no problems admitting he was over his head, but it wasn't in his nature to be a defeatist.

Brian grabbed the end of his T-shirt and lifted it up, wiping sweat off his forehead. Even with all the windows open, he was roasting. It was the middle of summer and they had to pick the hottest weekend of the month to move. No wonder Diane was so grumpy lately.

He grabbed yet another box labeled "living room" and tore the packing tape off the top. Throw cushions. Fabulous. He grabbed the first one and tossed it behind him, aiming for the couch but not really caring where it landed. Beneath that were paper-wrapped bowls and vases. Brian glanced around the room, wondering where he was going to put everything. He knew Diane had a place for every single item in these boxes, but seriously?

As he unwrapped a white handblown glass vase he'd bought as an anniversary gift one year, the front doorbell sounded, followed by three loud knocks. He stepped to the side to look out their large bay window and saw a black SUV in their driveway.

He recognized the vehicle. If his boss was making house calls, the day was about to go downhill fast.

"Door's open," Brian yelled across the room. He continued to unwrap the contents of the box while Tim Wainright walked into his house.

"How's it going?"

Brian shrugged, glanced around the box-filled room, and then smiled as Tim lifted up the case of beer in his hands.

"Housewarming gift."

Brian stepped over some boxes and lifted the beer from his boss's hands.

"You have no idea how much I needed this." He led the way through the hallway to the kitchen, set the box down on the counter, and reached for a drawer for a bottle opener, only to stop midway. "I have no clue where the bottle opener would be."

Tim reached for a bottle and twisted off the cap before handing it over with a smile. "I learned this trick the last time we moved. FYI, the bottle opener is always the last thing you'll find."

Brian tipped back his beer and enjoyed the cool liquid as it slid down his throat.

"So, are you here to shoot the breeze or do you feel like unpacking?" He swiped at his mouth and set the bottle down.

Tim he shook his head. "Are you nuts? I paid someone to unpack our place the last time. Almost saved our marriage too. Moving is stressful, especially when you have a hormonal pregnant wife. Where is she, by the way?" He leaned his elbows down on the counter and glanced around.

Brian groaned. "At the spa. And seriously, you paid someone?"

"Yeah." Tim laughed. "They offered a package I couldn't refuse. I'm surprised they didn't include it for you."

"They did." Brian's lip quirked with the admission.

"And you turned it down?"

Brian shrugged. That much was obvious. Maybe he could call them see if they could add it back on at the last minute? Wouldn't Diane be surprised if she came home to find most of the unpacking completed?

"Listen, I came here for a reason."

Brian took another swig of his beer and waited for the ball to drop. He knew it.

"I don't think Marie is working out. We're getting complaints from the London office."

That wasn't what he was expecting. Of course Marie was working out. He talked to her all the time, walking her through anything that popped up that she couldn't handle.

"Why is this the first I've heard this? I'm in touch with her daily, Tim. She's doing fine. Not even a hiccup. Everything is on track. Where's this coming from?"

The look on Tim's face took Brian aback. He could tell this was a struggle for his boss and that he didn't necessarily agree with what he was asking. Wouldn't be the first time Tim had to do the dirty work for William Harper, the COO of Harper and Wainright.

"I see. No need to say more." Brian sighed. He knew he'd already lost the battle.

Tim shrugged. "William would feel more comfortable if you were heading this up instead of Marie."

That was what he figured.

"What about my no-travel request until after the baby is born?"

Tim shook his head. "I'll make sure that it's not extensive."

Brian's fist clenched. "Even one week is too much. Come on, Tim, this is the least you could do for me." His original reasoning wasn't really valid; he wasn't concerned about Diane anymore. The pregnancy had so far been without complications, and other than the oddly intense mood swings, Diane literally glowed. She was happy and was even excited about their baby's arrival. He couldn't wait till they went furniture shopping for the nursery. But he wouldn't be able to do that for her, with her, if he wasn't here. And here was where he wanted to be. No questions asked.

"Will would just like you to head over there, take a look at things, and make sure everything is okay. He trusts you. If you say it's good, then he'll calm down."

"I've already said everything was good." Brian crossed his arms and leaned back. He knew he'd have to go if Tim insisted, but he'd make sure it wasn't without a fight.

"The main concern is that she's not telling you everything. Please? Go for a week. That's it. Take a look at the systems in place, talk to the staff, work with her hands-on a bit, and then come back with a glowing report. Diane's halfway through her pregnancy, right?"

Brian nodded. "She's just under thirty weeks."

"So you've still got time. Take a week to finish unpacking, then head over there."

Brian sighed. Diane wasn't going to be thrilled when she found out. She'd originally argued with him about his decision not to travel, but the further along she got in her pregnancy, the more she seemed to appreciate having him around. How was he going to tell her he was about to leave and that it might be for longer than he wanted? He knew Tim and William—when they said something would only take a week it usually ended up taking three.

"I really don't have a choice, do I?"

CHAPTER SIXTEEN

Diane

Present–June

M ake it stop. Please make it stop." I barely made any sound
with my plea and yet the pounding in my head tripled. I
couldn't move; there was a heaviness to my body that left
me unable to even shift slightly in my bed. The room was damp and I
couldn't stop shivering.

I was so tired.

"Can you take some water?"

The bed dipped as Nina sat beside me.

"I don't think I can move." I groaned as a wave of nausea hit me.

"On a scale of one to ten, how bad is it?"

I heard the rustle of pages being turned and the slight scratch of
a pen. She was recording all this. Again. Every day it seemed like she
needed to know how I was feeling, what I ate, how much I ate . . . I
complained about it, saying I didn't need a nursemaid, but she just
laughed and said once a nurse, always a nurse.

But I didn't need a nurse. I needed—

"Seven. Maybe an eight." I cracked open my eyes and the room
spun. "Oh God, Nina, I'm going to get sick." I forced myself up and
on my side, just in time to retch into the bowl Nina had ready for me.

I hated this.

"Why won't this stop?" I wiped my mouth and sank slowly back until my head rested on my pillow.

Nina placed a cold cloth on my forehead and I groaned in relief. At least three times a week this happened, and it was always after a pill Nina gave me the night before. A pill she said would help with my headaches.

"You're a liar," I whispered.

"I think it's time to rework your dosage. You're getting worse, not better," she muttered.

"How about we just stop the pills?" I cracked my eyes open again and caught the frown on her face.

"We can't do that. The withdrawal is too hard on your body. But we'll do a gradual decrease and see if that helps." She sat up and pulled up the covers. "Get some sleep now. I promise when you wake up, you'll feel much better."

"I can't do this anymore, Nina." I closed my eyes and sighed. I just wanted to sleep.

"Shhh. Try to sleep."

I turned my head and focused on my breathing. In and out. In and out. Voices drifted in as the door closed behind Nina leaving the bedroom. I just made out Charlie's voice.

"How is she today?"

"Better. I think it's working."

That caught my attention. Was that relief in Nina's voice? Didn't she just tell me she thought I was getting worse?

"Any mention of—"

"None."

"That's a first. That's . . ."

I couldn't hear anything else. Their voices drifted away as I lay there. The only sound I heard was the jackhammer in my head.

CHAPTER SEVENTEEN

Brian

September 2013

The wind blew across their path, stirring up the leaves in its wake.

Hand in hand, Brian and Diane headed down their street. It was a nightly ritual they'd started, these evening walks. All they needed was a dog to join them, and they'd blend right in with the rest of their neighbors. He'd mentioned it last night while they were in the park and Diane said she'd think about it.

For the first time since they'd been married, she hadn't laughed at the suggestion.

On his way home from work today, he'd noticed a new coffee shop that had opened a few blocks down and suggested they walk down and try it out tonight.

"Hey, neighbor." A head popped up from beneath the hood of a car. "Car troubles?"

Brian liked their neighbor of two doors down. They'd met Chad and his wife, Natasha, earlier in the summer at the community garage sale.

Chad scratched the top of his bald head.

"One year I'd like to own a car that doesn't give me problems." His lips twisted while he wiped his hands on a cloth.

Diane snickered and Brian caught what she'd seen. Chad had grease on his hands and his forehead was covered with it.

"Um . . ." Brian pointed to Chad's head.

Chad glanced at his hands and shrugged. He scrubbed at his forehead but it only smudged the grease.

"Tash?" he yelled over his shoulder.

"What's up?" Natasha, his wife, rounded the corner and started to laugh once she saw her husband.

Brian looked down at Diane and they both smiled.

While Chad looked like a big ox with his large stomach and tree trunk arms, his wife was a dainty piece of china who barely reached his shoulder.

"Are you trying to make us look like rednecks? It's bad enough you keep buying junkers to fix up. Do you need to look like one?" Natasha groaned as she came outside. She bypassed her husband and headed down to the sidewalk.

"It's a beautiful night for a walk, isn't it?" Natasha reached out for Diane's hand. "I've been meaning to come over with some baked goods, but Chad said that made me look too desperate." Natasha shrugged. "So, I figured I'd wait till you were home one day and invite you over for coffee."

"Coffee would be nice." Diane smiled and leaned into Brian.

He wrapped his arm around her. He really wanted them to make friends here. More important, he wanted Diane to make some friends. Women she could chat with over coffee and swap baby stories with.

"Hey, buddy, how are you?" Chad grabbed Brian's hand and crushed it.

Brian knew right away Chad would be a guy to relax with. From the overalls to the beer belly to the bandana stuck in the back pocket of the overalls, the guy reeked of grease and sweat. In a good way. It would be nice to have a friend who wasn't in the corporate world, who didn't wear a suit and tie every day, and who wouldn't talk incessantly about the newest computer software on the market.

"Are you a tinkerer?" Chad asked.

Brian grimaced at the thought but Diane answered for him.

"Only when it comes to computers."

"Ahh." Chad nodded. "A computer nerd. Gotcha."

Brian shrugged and glanced at their house and yard. Chad must have a nice comfy job to afford this place. It was larger than theirs.

Natasha slapped Chad on the arm. "And what do you call yourself?" Her arms crossed over her small chest as she glared up at her husband.

Brian had to bite his tongue to keep the smile off his face.

"A computer geek with attitude." Chad winked over at Brian before he placed both hands on his wife's cheeks and kissed her.

Brian chuckled. He never would have taken Chad as working in the same field as him.

"Where are you guys headed?" Chad asked.

Brian glanced down the street but Diane cut him off before he could speak.

"There's a new coffee shop we're going to check out. Care to join us?"

Natasha beamed a huge smile but shook her head. "I just took an apple pie out of the oven. Why don't you join us for a slice instead?"

"Oh, wait a minute now." Chad glared at his wife. "You'd better have made more than one pie if you're going to be offering my dessert to everyone on the street."

Brian caught the twinkle in his eye. "Come on now, what's a little pie between neighbors?" He couldn't help but tease.

A teasing glint appeared in Chad's eyes just before Natasha nudged him in the ribs to keep him quiet.

"If you're sure we're not putting you out?" Diane glanced up at Brian. He smiled down at her. He couldn't have planned this night any better if he'd tried.

A full stomach and an hour later, Brian was in Chad's garage pretending to admire the engine Chad was obviously working on. Brian had never been mechanically inclined and had no idea what Chad was talking about, but he nodded and grunted in what he hoped were the appropriate places.

"I imagine you do a lot of traveling in your position?" Chad's unexpected question caught Brian by surprise.

"A bit. Why?"

Chad slammed the hood down and leaned against the grille.

"I left my last job because of that. I couldn't handle the travel. I got tired of sleeping in lumpy hotel beds and eating fried food all the time." He rubbed his belly. "Although you wouldn't know it."

Brian knew the feeling all too well. "So, what do you do now?"

"Same thing, just no travel. I own a consulting company now and have a good team. We work with small companies that can't afford an in-house tech."

Impressed, Brian got Chad to talk more about his company and how he'd gone about setting it up. One day he might do the same. One day.

"Listen, with the baby coming, if you ever need us to keep an eye on your place or help out, just let us know. I know what it's like to not be around when your wife calls at two in the morning with a flooded kitchen."

Brian didn't know what to say.

"I mean it, buddy. We're here if you need us." Chad slapped Brian on the shoulder. "Come on, if we don't get back in there, the girls will start planning double dates for us."

When they entered the kitchen, Diane's face had gone pale white and he caught the small shake of her hands as she lifted the coffee mug to her lips.

"What's wrong?"

Natasha glanced over to them, stricken. "I'm so sorry. I thought you knew."

"Knew what?" Brian rushed over to Diane and placed his hands on her shoulders. He could feel her body shake beneath his touch. She wasn't one to normally get rattled, so it worried him.

"The baby's room . . . the baby died." Diane looked up at him, her eyes brimming with tears. "The baby died." She blinked and tears trickled down her face.

"Oh God, Tasha. Why did you have to tell her?" Chad groaned.

"I thought they knew. I'm so sorry."

Brian heard her apology but he didn't respond. He was too focused on Diane. He knelt beside her and took her hands. They were frozen. He rubbed them, trying to get the blood circulating to warm them up.

"Diane, honey. It's okay. Why don't we go home and get you into a nice hot bath? You're freezing." When she gripped his hand hard, he winced.

"Brian, the baby died in that house. And the mother got so depressed they had to move just to get away from the reminder. What if that happens to our baby?" Her eyes closed and her body swayed. Brian's anxiety level rose at the thought of her passing out.

"Come on, baby. Let's get you home." He put his arm around her and helped her stand.

"We never should have moved here," she whispered against him as he led her out of the house.

"It's going to be okay. Don't even think that way. It's all going to be okay." Brian tried to comfort her. He ignored his own misgivings as they walked up to their front porch.

How could he not know? How could the Realtor not tell him? He never would have bought the house otherwise.

As he helped Diane up the stairs and got her bathwater ready, an overwhelming sense of guilt ate at him. What could he do now? How could he make this better?

The paleness of her skin and the shivers that took over her body told him there was nothing he could do.

CHAPTER EIGHTEEN

Diane

Present–July

This little piggy went to market, this little piggy stayed home."
I wiggled Grace's toes and sang to her. She stared up at me,
her eyes wide and full of joy. The most precious smile I'd ever
seen stretched across her face as her tiny hands reached out.

All I wanted to do today was be a mom. From the moment I woke
up, I knew this was the right decision for me. To be here, with Grace.
Nothing else mattered.

It was amazing, really. I felt lighter, in control, and for the first day
in weeks, I had no headache.

It was going to be a good day. I knew it.

"Come on, sweet angel, let's go sit outside." I couldn't wait to feel
the sun on my skin. Lately, my hands were always freezing, and no
matter how thick my sweater, I just couldn't get warm.

With Grace in my arms, I made my way down the stairs. I couldn't
wait until she was old enough to walk down them herself. I could
almost picture her tiny fingers holding on to the railing as she took one
step at a time. I wanted to hear her laughter in the house and listen to
her footsteps as she ran down the hallway, with a puppy chasing after
her. I thought of the birthdays we'd celebrate here, the Christmas trees
decorated with her handmade ornaments.

It didn't hit me until we were almost at the kitchen that in none of those instances did I imagine Brian with us.

"Yes, I know what today is . . . I still think a separation at this time is too soon."

I stopped as Nina's voice carried down the hallway.

"Yes, I understand. I agree. It's why I'm here, after all."

Grace started to stir in my arms. I rocked her slightly while rubbing her back to soothe her. The last thing I wanted was for her to alert Nina to our presence. I had a feeling she was speaking to Brian. Who else could it be?

"Let's see how today goes first. I'll keep you informed."

Grace fussed all the more and I knew Nina would have heard her.

"Shh, little one. You're okay." I headed into the kitchen and decided to act as if I had overheard nothing.

"Good morning, Diane." Nina placed her phone in her pocket as I walked into the room. "Can I get you something to drink? Another cup of coffee, maybe?"

I turned Grace around so she faced Nina in hopes that would soothe her. She started to fuss in earnest now, and her whimpers bothered me.

"She's been like this all morning, Nina. Is this normal? Could she be teething?"

Nina barely gave Grace a glance. "Perfectly normal. Now, would you like a cup of tea or coffee?"

I ground my teeth at Nina's ignorance. Really? What, because I was home today, she focused on me only and not Grace? What kind of a nanny was she?

Maybe it was time for me to take more of an active part in Grace's daily routine. Time to cut the apron strings, so to speak. I really wasn't sure if I wanted to go back into work full time in the near future, so the need for a nanny wasn't as necessary as it had been before. Knowing Walter, I could probably convince him to let me work from home until Grace was old enough to go to day care.

"Nina, what's your usual routine? Since I plan to be home more often now, I'd like to keep it similar so as not to upset Grace too much." I kept my voice light, safe . . . even though if Nina bothered to look me in the eyes she'd know she was on dangerous ground.

"Your schedule. Yes, let's talk about that a bit. I think it needs some adjusting." She poured coffee into a mug and handed it to me. "Are you sleeping enough at night?"

"I think so. I've just got a lot on my mind."

I turned Grace around and tempted her with a pacifier. When she started to suck on it heavily, I realized she must be hungry. And yet, Nina was supposed to have fed her an hour ago.

"Could she be going through a growth spurt, maybe? I think she's hungry. Again. Didn't you just feed her?" I laughed, as if I found the idea funny that my child could be hungry. "Do you have more bottles made up?" I headed to the fridge and glanced inside. Empty. Why didn't she have any made up?

"I wish you had never talked me into letting my milk dry up." The memory was cloudy, but I remember never having felt so much pain and discomfort as in those first few days when my milk dried. The medication I was on helped, but that pain, of being engorged and knowing there was no relief, of listening to my baby cry and not being able to hold her until after she'd been fed . . . it was agony.

I wished I could remember the first few days of Grace's life. Instead, they were shadows in my mind. There were so many firsts I had missed out on—or at least didn't remember taking part in—and no photos. How could I have no photos of Grace's first days?

I searched the cupboards for bottles but couldn't find them.

"Did you rearrange the kitchen? Why can't I find anything I'm looking for?" I glanced over my shoulder. It was a little awkward trying to hold Grace while searching the cupboards.

"What are you looking for?" Nina sighed.

"Bottles." My shoulders tensed up and I could feel the twinges of another headache starting. No. Not today. Today was supposed to be a perfect day, with no issues. Just Grace and me. I let out a long, deep breath and kissed the top of Grace's head.

"I thought maybe we'd sit outside on the deck while I feed Grace, since it's so beautiful out."

This caught Nina's attention.

"And maybe go for a walk tonight after dinner when Charlie gets back," I added. Charlie had left early this morning to run some errands.

Nina smiled. I felt like the cat trying to lure the mouse into a trap. Except I had a feeling I underestimated the mouse.

"Now, that sounds like the best idea I've heard all day. You go on out and I'll make up a tray."

I glanced down at Grace, who sucked eagerly at her pacifier. Her eyes were closed and it looked as if she could nod off at any time, which might be a good thing. If I stretched out her feedings, it might make it easier to keep to her schedule.

"Don't worry, sweetheart. Mommy's home now and will take good care of you."

———

I wrapped my housecoat tight around me and made my way to the loft, where a girls' night was about to begin. Charlie had come home a little while ago after a day of running errands and suggested a movie and popcorn.

"So, what are we in the mood to watch?" Charlie sat on the couch, legs curled under her. On the coffee table in front of her was an assortment of snack food, everything from popcorn to chips to brownies and even my favorite cupcakes.

"When did you get those?" My eyes had lit up at the sight. A tray of the most succulent, decadent buttercream cupcakes I've ever tasted. It'd been so long since I last had one of those cupcakes—since before Grace was born, I think.

"While I was out. Figured we deserved to treat ourselves." She reached for one and placed it on a plate.

"What's the occasion?" I sat down beside her and pulled a blanket over my lap. Once again, I couldn't get warm.

"No reason," Charlie hedged while she handed me my plate.

I didn't buy it. It was our tradition only to get cupcakes when we had something to celebrate or to discuss.

"What's going on?" On edge now, I placed the plate with my cupcake down on the seat beside me.

When Charlie took a bite and refused to look me in the eye, I knew something was wrong.

"Do you remember how Mags used to tell us that if we let our hearts lead us in life, we could never go wrong?"

I nodded. It was Mags's favorite saying.

"Do you think we've done that?"

I shrugged. "I think we have to the best of our ability. Don't you?"

"Sometimes I wonder."

I looked at Charlie, really looked at her. The dark circles were still evident beneath her eyes, just like when she'd first arrived. She was a slender woman to begin with, but her cheekbones were more pronounced, her collarbone more distinct.

"Charlie, is something wrong? Are you sick? Is there something going on that you haven't told me about?" A million possibilities swirled in my head, and I knew if I could just reach up and pluck one of them out among the masses, I would know what was going on.

When she didn't respond, the hairs on the back of my neck stood at attention.

"Are you leaving?" The thought set my heart racing. I wasn't ready for her to leave me. I couldn't handle another person abandoning me.

"What? No. I promised I'd stay as long as you needed me."

"Explain the cupcake then." I settled in. Whatever it was that she wanted to discuss, I wanted her to know I was open to it. How bad could it be?

A sheepish grin crept on her face for a few moments before it disappeared. She set her plate back down on the coffee table and reached for my hand.

"Have you looked through the box I brought yet?"

I was really hoping she would have forgotten about that box. I could have lied and said I hadn't looked through it yet, but . . .

"You don't really want to talk about it, do you?

"What's there to talk about? Are you really wanting to rehash our childhood again?"

"I'd like to talk about this." She bent down and picked up something from the floor.

I watched as she reached into her purse and pulled out a book I would always instantly remember.

The book itself was nondescript. A soft yellow cover that had faded with age. But it was a journal that I had kept secret from both my sister and my aunt, the one in which I tried to understand our parents' actions and how they had molded me into an adult.

But that wasn't the only reason why I had kept it secret. I let out a long sigh and held out my hand. It took her a moment, but she released it to me.

"Please tell me you didn't read it." I knew that was wishful thinking by the way her chin dropped to her chest.

It really wasn't the words written inside the journal that I didn't want her to read, but what was contained between the pages. I'd placed the note our mother had written right before she killed herself in there; the note I had kept from Charlie for all these years.

She shook her head. "I didn't read your journal. We promised each other we wouldn't."

Relieved, I held out my hand for the book, but she pulled it closer and opened it, flipping through the pages.

"I did find this, however." She pulled it out and held it up.

I didn't know what to say, how to explain . . . nothing I would have said would make up for what was written on that note.

Nothing.

"Why didn't you burn this? Why keep it as a reminder? Why torture yourself like this?"

"I couldn't." I smoothed the blanket that was on my lap and picked at stray pieces of lint. "Those words were the last things Mom said. I didn't . . . I couldn't . . ." I struggled to find the words to explain.

"I would have." There was a harsh determination in Charlie's voice. "I would have been okay remembering how Mom was that morning when we said good-bye. How she gave me an extra hug and kissed the top of my forehead, how she smelled, and the slight whiff of coffee on her breath. I would have been okay with that. I would have remembered her last words to me for the rest of my life and forgotten all about this note. She told us she loved us." Charlie wiped at the tears pooling in her eyes. "Do you remember that? That she loved us more than life."

Of course I remembered that. How could I forget?

"She lied, didn't she?" Charlie looked away from me. "I never thought about that until now. That she lied to us. Did she know that morning what she was going to do or was it a decision she made later? Did she even think about us, how it would affect us?"

I reached my hand out to touch her. I could hear in her voice how much this ate at her.

"She never lied to us, Charlie. You have to believe that."

Charlie snorted.

"I do." I wasn't just saying that either. I really did believe it.

"How? How could you believe that?"

My world stood still for just a second before a moment of clarity hit me hard. I almost reeled from the impact.

Charlie wasn't afraid of the hormonal imbalance she might or might not experience if she ever had a child. Postpartum psychosis wasn't the nightmare in her sleep. It was the abandonment. That was what scared her the most.

And it was in that moment that my own fears of being crazy were wiped clean. I knew I wasn't. I couldn't be. I'd faced the one thing that scared me the most and I walked away whole.

I did, didn't I?

I jumped up from the couch and went to go check on Grace.

"Diane, what are you doing?" Charlie called out to me.

"One minute," I softly called over my shoulder. I nudged the door to Grace's bedroom open and peeked in. The hallway light arched in the room until it highlighted the crib, enough so I could see her legs twitching. I tiptoed in and gazed down at her. The shadows played with her face, but there was enough light to show me what I needed to see. The way her lips puffed out with each breath and the rise of her chest as she took in air.

"I love you, angel," I whispered.

"Diane?" Charlie stood at the door and watched me.

"I thought I heard something," I hedged.

I followed her back to the couch and we sat there in silence. I picked up the note from our mother and opened it, smoothing out the crease down the center.

"Remember when you first arrived and we talked about Mom? I said she couldn't cope, but you said it was postpartum psychosis."

Charlie nodded.

"So, it's possible she wasn't in the right frame of mind when she wrote this note, correct?"

Charlie just stared at me.

"Aunt Mags told us it was like a switch went off in her brain and her entire world changed within moments. That's what happens, right?" Mags would know. As a nurse, she had worked with many new mothers—she'd know the signs, know what to look for, and understand what it all meant.

Charlie withdrew from me at that point. She pulled back, arms crossed as she stared at the baby monitor I'd placed on the coffee table.

"Sometimes. Other times it's a gradual change, something most people wouldn't recognize until it was too late," she muttered.

"How could most people not recognize it? I mean, I know we were kids, we weren't going to notice it, but Dad should have, right?"

Charlie shook her head. A blanket of sadness weighed her down; I could see it in the droop of her shoulders and the shadow in her eyes as she finally looked at me.

"Ignorance is bliss. Those who are closest want to ignore the signs, blame it on something else if they can." She tilted her back to rest on the couch. "It's easier, or so we tell ourselves. Just give it time, it'll all work out. One day at a time, that's what Walter said. One day at a time. But it's so hard." Her voice drifted off.

"Charlie?" I swallowed hard past the lump in my throat. Did something happen, something more than just an ultimatum from Marcus that brought her back home?

She turned toward me and smiled. "Enough melodrama. I need to head out for a few days. My boss called and they'd like me to head down to Texas to help train a new team that leaves at the end of the week. I won't be gone long."

"What? I thought you weren't leaving?" She couldn't go. Not now. Not yet. I wasn't ready. I hid my trembling hands beneath my legs and struggled to put a smile on my face. I didn't want her to know how panicked I felt.

"It's only for a few days. I'll be back before you know it."

"What if Grace and I came with you?" The words rushed out before I even had the chance to think. I wanted to take them back the instant I said them, not only because of the rejection in Charlie's face but also because there was no way I could take Grace anywhere now, anyway, not after she had almost gotten run over.

"Oh, honey, I . . . that wouldn't work. I'll be . . . crazy busy."

"No, no, it's okay." I swept my hair back behind my head and fiddled with the blanket over my lap.

"Hey, if we don't start the movie soon I'm going to head off to bed." I exaggerated my yawn.

Charlie smiled and reached for the remote. With her occupied, I sneaked the note I still held in my hand into my pants pocket.

I hated that she'd read it. Hated that it had affected her in a way she couldn't admit to. Hated that there was nothing I could do to help her. Was that why she was leaving after she said she would stay as long as I needed her?

"You will come back, won't you?" I struggled to keep the insecurity out of my voice, but even I could hear it.

Charlie reached across the couch, grabbed my hand, and squeezed. "I'll be here for as long as you need me. I promise."

I smiled, reassured in the knowledge that I wouldn't be left alone.

Except, no matter how many promises someone made to me, I always ended up alone. Always.

CHAPTER NINETEEN

I t was midafternoon, and while I knew I really should put Grace down for her nap, I had a sudden urge to get out.

I wasn't sure whether it was the fact that both Nina and Charlie had left earlier in the morning and I was wandering aimlessly around the house or whether I was just ready to get out.

There was only one place that didn't fill me with a sense of panic when I thought of taking Grace out on my own. It would mean my first trip with her, but it was time.

Time for me to step up and be the type of mother I should be. I couldn't hide my daughter anymore; there was no need to. There was no big bad wolf out there just waiting to snatch her from me. The realization was liberating.

I felt guilty as I snuck us out of the house, but it wasn't like I was housebound. I could come and go as I pleased. And it pleased me to leave at that very moment.

At the same time, I knew I was being sneaky. I did leave a note on the kitchen counter for Nina just in case. Better to ask forgiveness than permission, right?

The moment I pulled up into the restaurant's parking lot I knew I'd done the right thing. I should have come here days or even weeks ago. I should have suggested it to Charlie. She loved coming here. Maybe when she came back we would plan a girls' night out.

"Diane!"

Marcello greeted me with open arms the moment I walked through the door. He brought me close and squeezed tight, laughing as he kissed both my cheeks.

"Bella, I've missed you. You don't call, you don't come in . . . how am I to take care of you when you don't come?" He grabbed my hand and pulled me behind him.

I pulled back.

"Wait. I want to introduce you to someone. You're the first of my friends to officially meet her." I held up the baby carrier and pulled back the blanket that covered Grace.

"Marcello, meet my little angel. Grace, meet the man who will teach you to love all things Italian."

Tears gathered in Marcello's eyes as he saw Grace for the first time. He blinked his lashes a few times before turning to give me another hug.

"Oh, sweet darling." It was all he said, but I could see the love for her in his face.

"I know I should have brought her in sooner, but . . ." I gave him a sheepish smile as he held my hand and walked me into my little sitting area.

I gazed around me and sighed. Yes, this was what I needed.

"Can I get you some wine? Are you allowed? Or maybe some sparkling water?"

"Wine. White, please." It felt like ages since I'd last had a glass of wine. I knew I probably shouldn't have any with the medication I was on, but at the moment, I didn't care.

"Chardonnay?"

I nodded.

I placed Grace down beside me before I sat in the small chair I'd picked out for this area. I watched her, the way her lashes kissed her cheeks, and the way her lips relaxed into a smile as she slept. She really was my angel.

On the other side of me was a small table with books I'd picked up from secondhand stores. An old hardback book with no cover was on top. I picked it up and smiled. This was definitely not one of mine.

"Ah, I see you found my latest secret."

I glanced up to find Marcello in front of me, holding out a glass of wine.

I tipped the book over before putting it back down. *Alice in Wonderland.* I couldn't help but smile.

"It's our little secret," I promised. I thought Marcello might read some of the books I brought in, even use this small area as his own. Now I knew I had been right.

I took a sip of the wine, ignoring all the warnings blaring through my mind, and thoroughly savored the smooth liquid as I rolled it around my tongue.

Marcello pulled up a chair and sat opposite me. He glanced down at Grace before he leaned forward and reached for my free hand.

"I've been worried about you. Things haven't been the same here with you not coming by for my pasta . . . I wanted to see you, but . . ." He patted my hand before letting go.

"It's taken me a little bit longer than I thought it would to get back to my daily routine." I shrugged. "If I even knew what that was anymore."

"Ahh, it takes time. Don't be so hard on yourself." He glanced down at Grace. I followed his gaze, my heart bursting with love once again as I watched her. It surprised me how much this happened to me. I used to laugh when I would hear stories of young mothers who couldn't stop talking about their babies. Now I knew. Now I understood.

"Did you know Charlie was back at home?" It had become a tradition for Charlie and me to come here and say good-bye before she left for her latest assignment with Doctors Without Borders. She would always load up on carbs and claimed no one could make a cream sauce like Marcello.

"Yes, yes. She came in yesterday for a plate of carbonara. She doesn't look well, that girl. My heart worries for her." Marcello covered his chest with his hand.

Of course she did. One more thing she did on her day out yesterday that she excluded me from.

"I think she's just tired. She doesn't take many breaks in between her missions."

"Well, I love that she's staying closer to home for a while. Give me time to put some meat on her bones. Which reminds me, now that you're here, you'll let me do what I promised, yes?"

I took another sip of my wine.

"What do you mean, 'what you promised'?"

Marcello pushed himself up from his chair.

"It breaks my heart that I broke my word. But I'll make it up." He leaned down and kissed my hand. "Now, sit back and just relax. Enjoy your wine."

I watched as he walked into the back area and wondered what he meant.

I could only assume he meant Brian. He must have made Marcello promise to take care of me as only Marcello could do.

Once, when I was sick, Marcello had made some homemade chicken soup for Brian to pick up for me. Another time, when we moved into our new place, he'd called Brian to let him know our dinner was ready.

I thought back to the conversation I'd overheard earlier from Nina. I kept thinking about what kind of separation she was talking about, and why now wouldn't be the right time. It didn't make sense.

If she was talking to Brian, there could only be one answer.

But what if she was talking to someone else? What kind of separation? Not from Grace. Why would she take my daughter away from me?

Tonight, maybe during our walk or afterward, when we had tea, I needed to have a talk with Nina. I needed answers. It was one thing if she had been in contact with my husband and didn't tell me, but it was quite another thing if she planned to take my child away from me.

"I hope you've been craving this. You are too thin. You need to promise to come in more so I can fatten you up." Marcello appeared to the side and held a plate in his hands.

A waiter brought over a small table to place in front of me. He covered it with a tablecloth, candleholders, and silverware. Once he was done, Marcello set the small plate of bruschetta down before he added a vase with a rose to the table.

"I don't need the fancy china." I smiled at him. I realized it had felt like ages since I'd last been hungry, but all of a sudden I was starved.

"You, my beautiful lady, deserve only the best." He bowed and blew me a kiss.

One bite of the bruschetta and I was in heaven. The garlic, tomatoes, and basil blend on the bread was the best thing I'd eaten in ages. This was the way a person should eat, with flavors that exploded with each bite. The Italian way.

"Grace, one day you and I will cook like this in our kitchen. Your father and I used to cook for each other. I'm not sure if we ever will again, but it's in your blood." She slept, but I believed she could still hear my voice. I knew it from the way she'd often smile in her sleep when I would talk to her.

"I hope you're hungry." Marcello's loud voice boomed in the empty room. I'd just realized I was the only one there.

He brought a large bowl of angel hair pasta with chicken covered in Alfredo sauce. The waiter behind him carried a cheese grater for the best Parmesan cheese I'd ever tasted. I almost groaned in ecstasy.

"I hope you're going to join me," I said. There was too much pasta in that bowl for one person.

The waiter set another place at the table but Marcello only shook his head.

"No, but I will." A hand squeezed my shoulder. I glared at Marcello, who had the grace to look away.

Why was Nina here?

―――

"I'm sorry, Diane. I called Nina to come and join you."

He must have caught the deadly look in my eyes. He lifted his hands and shrugged. I wasn't really too surprised that she showed up. It wasn't like I kept my plans a secret. I did leave a note telling her where I was.

"I've wanted to meet her for a long time," Marcello said.

I just stared at him.

"And you shouldn't be eating alone. It's not right." He looked down toward Grace. "Not now."

"What does that mean?" The sound of my fork dropping on my plate carried through the restaurant. Marcello cringed.

"He means"—Nina left my side and sat down in the chair opposite of me—"we both know how hard today must be, and you shouldn't have to be alone."

"What's so hard about today?"

"Because it's your anniversary." There was a look in Nina's eyes, like she was sizing me up and waiting to see how I'd react.

I shook my head. They were wrong.

"Did you forget?" Nina's voice lowered.

I blinked as my eyes welled with tears. Today wasn't my anniversary. It couldn't be. That was still months away, wasn't it? I wouldn't forget my anniversary; I knew I wouldn't.

"It can't be." I wiped at the tears that flowed down my cheeks. My mind was blank. Our anniversary was in July. And this was . . . there was still time, wasn't there?

"How could I forget our anniversary? How could Brian forget? Where is he? Why isn't he here?" I shook my head, my gaze frozen on my plate as I tried to process this.

Our last anniversary had been perfect, the best night of my life in years. Brian and I always planned how we would celebrate together, and normally we'd either go away for the weekend or go out for dinner. But for our twelfth, no, thirteenth anniversary it was different. We both had to work late, so we'd agreed to celebrate it on the weekend, but that night Brian surprised me by taking me out to a five-star restaurant we'd both wanted to try but could never get reservations for. But instead of a regular meal in the dining area, Brian had called in a favor and we had been seated at the chef's table in the kitchen.

It was a night made of dreams. We were both drunk on love, and the food was our foreplay.

How could I have forgotten what today was?

"Nina?" Stricken, I looked to Nina for help.

She leaned forward and reached for my hands. I swallowed hard, not realizing how much this would hurt. This. All of it. My memory loss, the panic attacks, the way my mind played tricks on me. And where was Brian? Why the silence? Why did he leave me? Oh God, he left me, didn't he? That was why he hadn't come home. That was why it had only been Nina who'd talked to him. That was why she thought today would be so hard for me. He left me and I was all alone. Till death do us part. What happened to that promise?

"I want to go home now." I sounded like a child as I whispered my plea. I needed to leave. I didn't understand the reason but it was all I could focus on. Home. My chest hurt; my heart raced as I reached for Grace and ignored Marcello, who stood there wringing his hands.

"Please? Please just take me home."

CHAPTER TWENTY

Brian

October 2013

M arie, you're a bit behind schedule. What can I do to help?"
Brian leaned back in his chair and crossed his arms
behind his head. He watched Marie on his computer
screen. She looked tired and worn out. He knew the eight-hour time
difference didn't help, and while he was only starting his day, she was
ready to end hers.

"Get William off my back?" She smiled but he heard the annoy-
ance in her voice. He winced. He knew exactly how she felt but there
was little he could do about it.

"He likes to be hands-on; you know that."

"I think taking this job was a mistake. I think you know that as
well. He doesn't trust me, and instead of helping me all he's doing is
hindering every step I take. How does he expect me to be on schedule
when he's the one holding me back?"

Nicole, Brian's assistant, stood at his door with a notebook in
hand. Brian glanced down at the time on his computer screen, then
held up his hand, requesting five more minutes.

"Recommending you was not a mistake. You just need to look outside the box. I know you think William's requests for continual updates

and approvals are slowing you down, but trust me, his only goal is to ensure your success."

From the look on Marie's face, Brian knew she could see right through him. She was smart, and he still trusted his gut that she could do this.

"Have you updated the task list lately? I noticed there were still items missing that I'm sure you've taken care of. Take a look, and tomorrow morning I'll go through it and see what I can help with on my end here. It'll also give me an idea of how I can help you when I come out there next week."

He waited for the bomb to drop.

"Are you firing me?" she asked after a few seconds of silence.

Brian fiddled with his pen.

"Why would you ask?" He hated to do this to her. He understood how she must be feeling. He'd been in her same shoes years ago.

"Why else would you be coming out to replace me?"

Brian read the acceptance in her eyes and he hated seeing it. He honestly thought she'd be perfect for this setup. He knew it would have its challenges, but it was a smaller office with fewer complications. He hadn't expected William to get so involved.

"No one said anything about replacement. I'm only coming out for a few days, a week at the most, to help smooth things out and ease William's mind."

"Ease . . ." Marie stumbled over the word.

Brian smiled in reassurance. Nicole stood outside his door again.

"Listen, go through the tasks and update everything for tomorrow, okay? Nicole will e-mail you my itinerary once it's booked. Stop worrying. Things will be fine. I've got your back."

He caught the quick blinking Marie tried to disguise. He said good-bye, disconnected their Skype session, and searched for the file he needed to bring with him to his next meeting.

"I've got it right here." Nicole held up the file. "I've also got a fresh cup of coffee waiting for you at your seat. I was able to book three more interviews today. Don't worry, I'll order you lunch."

Brian groaned. He'd been dreading this day for a while. He hated doing interviews. For years he'd argued that the HR department could handle this for him, but it was Tim who changed his mind-set, albeit begrudgingly on Brian's part. They had gone through too many newbies fresh from college who didn't know their way around a hard drive, before he realized that if he wanted to build a team that would work alongside him he needed more of a hands-on approach. So far it had worked. His revolving door of employees had lessened and he liked the team he worked with.

But Tim wanted him to expand, to broaden their portfolio. Thankfully, they had a friend who was a headhunter and Brian didn't have to go through hundreds of applications of home-taught tech professionals. After assessing the twenty applicants who seemed most promising, Brian had narrowed it down to five, with three positions available.

Instead of playing around with a new system they'd just installed for a department, he had to sit in a drab boardroom meeting potential coworkers who were dressed to cover up any inadequacies they thought they could hide.

What they didn't know was that Brian was a man who could see past facades. It was the one skill that didn't involve computers that he excelled at.

———

Brian walked into the bar two doors down from the office and squinted. Tim had sent him an e-mail telling him to come meet him for a drink, but Brian didn't see the guy.

He walked over to the bar and ordered a draft, then turned and surveyed the crowd. It was standing room only; men with loosened ties and women with unbuttoned suit jackets relaxed among their peers before heading home and facing another set of pressures.

Brian used to love this time of the day, but in all honesty, all he wanted to do these days was rush home to Diane. They'd been working on spending more quality time together, even to the point of setting aside two nights a week to take personal cooking lessons from Marcello. Those nights had become the highlight of his weeks.

"Brian!"

He heard his name being yelled from the back corner. He grabbed his beer and made his way through the crowd, keeping his mug high as he wove through the groups standing around.

Tim had managed to snag a table, and he wasn't alone.

William sat to one side, and across from him, beside an empty chair, sat Esther Price, the other partner in the firm.

Brian's hands began to sweat. This couldn't be good. The only time Esther ever got involved in anything was when something major was at stake.

Like his job, maybe?

"Sit, sit." William waved him to the empty seat. Brian smiled at Esther as he sat down but didn't say anything. He'd never really had a good relationship with the woman.

"How did the interviews go?" Tim broke the awkward silence while Brian took a sip of his beer.

"Not too bad. They're all great candidates. One might be a better fit in Marcia's department. She's worked as admin for departments in the past, and her skills would be better suited there. Perhaps as a backup for Nicole." He'd been trying to get Nicole help for a few years now. If his department's growth was to continue, they'd need more administrators or else Nicole would walk. She'd warned him moments before he left this evening.

Losing her was not an option. It was hard to train someone to meet your admin needs as perfectly as Nicole did. She'd be hard to replace.

"Great to hear. We were just talking about how well your department is doing." Tim leaned back in his chair. There was a look on his face that Brian couldn't read. His fingers tightened around his mug as he tried to understand whatever message Tim was sending, but he couldn't.

Everything inside of him screamed to run away.

"Have you given thought to finding someone to fill your role here at our home office, while you're at our other offices overseas?" Esther said.

"Do I need to?" He caught the emphasis on *offices*. He didn't like where this was headed.

Esther's lips tightened for a brief moment.

"I don't ask questions to waste time. I'd appreciate you considering that before giving me another flippant remark."

He was about to get fired. He knew it. He didn't know why, but all the signals were there. It was probably his own fault too. Diane warned him about this at the beginning, when he requested that he travel less. She had an inkling something like this would happen. She told him he needed to make a decision before he went to Tim about staying at home. That it was up to him if he wanted to keep his job or find something else. He hadn't thought it would come to that. He'd worked for Harper and Wainright LLC for far too long for them to sack him over something like asking for less travel time while his wife was pregnant.

Apparently, though, Diane had been right.

The right thing to do would be to kiss ass, even if it was the last thing he wanted. He liked this job and he wanted to keep it. Sure, he could find another job if he needed to. All it would take were a few feelers and he'd have an offer within a few hours. But there was a reason he continued to turn down the job offers that came across his desk on a regular basis. All those phone calls from friends at other companies, the e-mails from headhunters and lunch invitations from CEOs at other firm—none of them mattered to him. He was happy where he was. Content. Secure.

At least, he had been. He'd give anything to hit the rewind button and erase the last fifteen minutes.

"There's nothing flippant about my question, Esther. Do I need to find someone to fill my role? Up until now it was never an issue."

From the startled expression on Esther's face to the soft murmur from William, it was safe to assume they'd expected Brian to roll over and play dead for them.

"You're not getting fired."

Brian stared at Tim. "Are you sure? The last time someone in our office was asked to find a replacement, they were escorted out by security a few hours later."

He wasn't sure what type of game Tim was playing. Was he friend or boss?

"No one is getting fired, least of all you." William leaned close, forcing Esther to lean back, and smacked his hand down on the table. "You're too damn important to this company and you know it. That's the problem."

The problem? That didn't make sense to him at all. He took a deep drink of his beer, wiped his lips, and stared at his boss.

"This test of yours, planting Marie in the London office, just isn't going to work. She's good, I'll admit that, but I would feel a whole hell of a lot more comfortable if you were the one leading the team over there."

"I'm going next week."

"One week isn't going to be long enough. We're expanding and we need someone who knows what he's doing leading the pack. You can't do that from here." William leaned back, folded his arms over his massive chest, and grinned.

Brian wanted to wipe the grin off his face.

"What do you mean, I can't do it from here? I've set up all the other offices just fine." None of this was making any sense.

"Exactly."

Tim cleared his throat.

"Listen. What we're trying to say, albeit the wrong way, is that we want you to continue in your role in setting up our offices worldwide, but in a larger capacity. We need you to be in charge of it, to actually be there, in the offices, taking care of all the minute details, rather than overseeing it from your office here in the States."

Brian couldn't believe what he was hearing. Tim knew how he felt about this. He knew Brian didn't want to travel anymore, that he couldn't.

"What about my request to lessen the amount of travel I do now? I have a baby on the way. I'd like to be home to see him or her grow. I can't do that with the amount of travel I do. You know that." He glared at Tim.

Brian's body tensed. He should have listened to his instincts earlier and left. Why hadn't he? Nothing good was going to come out of this. How could he explain to Diane that he had to break his promise? That he wouldn't be the one to support her with their baby; that he was going to be an absentee father? It wasn't what he wanted. It wasn't what either of them wanted.

"Take her with you. We'd like you to make the London office your home. It'll be far less travel time to our other branches across Europe from there," Esther said.

His hands fisted in his lap. He envisioned himself slamming his fists down on the table and Esther's drink spilling all over her lap. He imagined the look of horror as her red wine stained her pressed linen skirt and the feeling of satisfaction that would fill him.

At the same time, this sudden explosion of rage inside of him was contradictory to who he was. He was the peacemaker, the one who saw both sides of the story. Where did all this emotion come from?

"I'm surprised you could say that, Esther. You've met my wife. She's dedicated to her job and wouldn't dream of leaving it to follow me halfway around the world." He was surprised at how calm his voice was when inside he was seething.

"Of course she wouldn't," William agreed. "But she'll be on maternity leave, so consider it a family vacation for the first little while. Things tend to work themselves out if you just give it time, and who knows, her company might want to think about expanding their own business overseas. What a perfect opportunity."

Brian grabbed his beer and downed it all, ignoring the way his hands shook. This was surreal. Diane was not going to leave her job, her company, and her life for him. He knew that. Tim knew that. It wasn't even a question.

"And if I say no?" He shouldn't have said that. He should have asked for a couple of days to think about it, to see if he could figure out a way to make it work.

Esther laughed, William smiled, and Tim shook his head.

"You can't," William said.

Of course he couldn't. He had a family to think about. He had a career to consider.

He could say no. There were plenty of other companies out there; he'd have a job in no time. Then he could do what he wanted to do the most—be at home with his family.

Standing up for himself wasn't in his nature. He was a behind-the-scenes kind of guy. He preferred it that way. Which was why he should thank them for this opportunity and head home to his wife.

Brian pushed back his chair and stood. He fingered his wedding ring, spinning it around his finger, and thought about the vows they'd made to each other outside of their ceremony all those years ago. Vows to never hinder each other's dreams, to always be there for support and encouragement. Brian didn't mind the thirty weeks each year that he traveled. Every time another project popped up on his task list, an expansion or an issue that required him to be hands-on, he got excited. The travel thrilled him. The jet lag never bothered him. The time away from home didn't concern him, because he knew Diane had his back. It was one of the strengths of their marriage. It was also one of the many reasons they'd agreed to wait ten years before they had children.

But times had changed. Now she was pregnant and he would need to be home more often. He took a deep breath. Family came first. Always.

"I can and I will. And if it's not acceptable to you, then I quit."

He turned and walked away. He heard William call him back but it didn't matter. With each step he took, Brian knew he was taking a step away from his job.

He might need to consider being a stay-at-home dad. God knew they didn't need his income. They could do fine on just Diane's.

He reached for the doorknob, his fingers tightening around it, and just as he was about to turn, a hand landed on his shoulder.

CHAPTER TWENTY-ONE

Brian turned to find Esther behind him.

"Don't leave, please. That didn't happen the way we'd thought it would. Come back to the table and let us explain."

Brian searched her eyes, surprised that she'd be the one to come and stop him. If anything, he would have expected Tim to be the one to talk him down from the ledge.

His body hummed with tension. He couldn't believe he'd just offered to quit. What was he thinking? He'd never quit a job like that. Ever. The process of leaving one job for another had always been well thought out and planned.

Back at the table, Tim stood as if waiting for him to return on his own accord, while William sat back in his chair with a shocked expression in his eyes.

"Just hear us out," Tim asked.

Brian sat down in the chair he had just left, leaned back, and waited.

"We don't want you to quit. What we want is to give you a promotion," Tim began.

Brian cocked his head. Did he hear him right? "A promotion?"

"President of international operations and communication." A slow smile spread across Tim's face.

Brian coughed. "President?"

William cleared his throat. "I'm very serious about trusting only you for this position. Please don't make me bring someone in with less talent."

He was speechless. This wasn't what he expected to hear. President? He never imagined he'd ever reach a position so high. He thought director of technology was as far as he could go. President. Him. How could he pass this up? How could he say no?

"I don't know what to say."

"Don't say anything. Not tonight. I know it's asking a lot, and that it might not be the right timing, but talk to your wife and let us know." William pushed his chair back and stood.

"I know we've had our differences in the past, but on this I agree." Esther stood as well, placing her hand on his shoulder and giving it a slight squeeze.

Brian sat there speechless, the wind knocked out of him as if he'd been sucker punched.

"I should have warned you." Tim flagged down a server and ordered two more beers.

Brian laughed, a sudden sound that came from deep in his chest. Yeah, he should have been warned, but would it have made a difference? He still couldn't take the job. He could never ask Diane to give up the life she'd worked so hard for.

"You know I can't take it." Defeat filled him at the thought. It was harder than expected to accept this new reality. The perfect job for him was within arm's reach and he had to turn it down.

"See, that's what I don't get. You're not even giving it a chance. Diane might surprise you," Tim said.

Brian shook his head.

Tim shrugged. "Okay, okay, you know your wife better than anyone else. But I still think you deserve to give yourself the chance. It's not like you need to stay there year-round. You can come back every month if you need to. We can make it work."

The server arrived and set the beers down in front of them.

"William wants to make it work." Tim raised his mug and waited for Brian to do the same.

Brian hesitated and he didn't know why. Knowing Tim supported him, that he thought it possible, meant something to him. But all he could think about was his wife and that baby he couldn't wait to meet. His entire life had changed the moment he found out Diane was pregnant. His priorities had been forever altered in that one instant.

"Would you leave your wife and kids and be content seeing them a few days each month?" Brian already knew how Tim would respond.

Tim lowered his glass and rubbed his face. "We lead different lives, you and I. This has been your goal for so long. It's not mine. I'm content being home and seeing my kids for an hour or so a night before they go to bed. Quality versus quantity. And let's be honest—a newborn really doesn't need the father. Hire some help for Diane, get a nanny to help with the diaper changes and night feedings. Are you honestly going to give up your dream job for that?"

Brian shrugged. "This caught me off guard."

"I know. William didn't expect you to react this way, obviously. He's been planning this for a while now."

Brian dropped his head back and groaned. "You couldn't have given me a hint or something?"

Tim shook his head. "I was under orders to keep quiet."

Brian took a long drink of his beer and enjoyed the rush of liquid as it trailed down his throat. He glanced at his watch and winced. He needed to get home. Diane had an ultrasound today and he had wanted to have dinner started before she arrived. That wasn't going to happen now. Might as well just order in.

"Let me think about it." He got to his feet.

Tim did the same. "Do more than just think about it. Talk with Diane."

Brian nodded in agreement. Sure, he'd mention it to her. But hell would freeze over before she left her job just so he could take this advancement.

It wasn't until he was walking toward the train station that he realized he'd gone from knowing he wouldn't take the job to hoping Diane would give him the okay to do so.

———

Brian entered the kitchen through the garage door and dropped the bags in his hand on the counter.

"Sorry I'm late," he called out. He'd texted Diane earlier, only to find out she was already home. When he asked what she was in the mood for she responded with one word: Chinese. It surprised him, especially after last week, when her feet, fingers, and legs started to swell right after eating it. She swore she wouldn't eat Chinese again.

"Are you hungry?" he called out. When there was no response, he went to check on her.

Diane sat on the couch, her feet propped up on the coffee table, with a box of Kleenex to the side. When she looked up at him, her red eyes were rimmed with unshed tears.

"Hey, what's wrong?" He sat down beside her and wrapped her in his arms. She laid her head on his chest and gave a deep sigh.

Diane wasn't one to cry. He could count on one hand the number of times he'd seen tears fall, and when she did, she made sure she was always alone.

She'd had her appointment today, but she hadn't said anything about it. Did something happen?

He gently rubbed her arms, hoping to calm her, unsure of what to do or how to do it. He tried to convince himself not to worry, that maybe she'd read a sad book or something. But when she snuggled into him, he knew it had to be something else. Something beyond pregnancy hormones.

"Are you okay? Is the baby okay?" He pulled back slightly to watch her face. She wouldn't raise her eyes. "What's wrong?"

He'd read stories online about complications during pregnancy, and years ago one of their friends had lost their child weeks before she was due to give birth. Every time the thought would try to creep in that something could go wrong, he'd quash it down. It wasn't possible. Not to them. Not to their child. Something like a fist formed in his chest, blocking his windpipe. No, damn it, not to their child. Not to his wife.

"Diane, speak to me." His hold on her tightened.

"Remember how we thought the swelling was from the Chinese last week? We were wrong." Her voice was dull.

Brian laid his hand over her protruding stomach and was relieved to feel a tiny kick.

"What is it then?"

"Preeclampsia."

From the flatness of her tone, to the way her face blanched, Brian took it to mean something as bad as death. Was she dying? Was their baby dying?

"What is that?"

She twisted out of his embrace and tucked her legs beneath her. Brian let her withdraw, more familiar with this side of his wife than the crying one.

"It means my body is rebelling. My placenta isn't working properly and it could affect the baby. My blood pressure is too high and I've been placed on bed rest. Bed rest! Brian, I can't do that. So what if there's iron in my urine. So what if my blood pressure is too high. Do they honestly think it's going to go down if I stay in bed all day?"

"So you're okay then? The baby is okay too?" Brian's head dropped back and he closed his eyes in relief. He had thought they were dying, for Pete's sake. Bed rest? High blood pressure? That was all?

"Yes, I'm okay. The baby is okay. Well . . . everything is fine for now. This is a precaution. An unnecessary one, if you ask me. I don't do bed rest, Brian; you know that. I tried explaining it to him, but he threatened to put me in the hospital otherwise." She rolled her eyes.

Brian wanted to shake her. This was their baby they were talking about. She should want to do everything she could to ensure their child was okay. So what if she had to spend a few weeks in bed. It might actually do her some good.

"I'm sure you don't have to actually be in bed. Just relaxing. Right?"

When she didn't respond, he opened his eyes to catch her glaring at him.

"What?"

"This isn't a good time for me. We just landed a contract I've been working on for months, Walter wants to go on vacation before I need time off, and I haven't found someone to fill in for me while I'm out. I'm not ready for this. Not yet."

Brian snorted.

"Don't be rude." Diane's lips pinched together.

She was right. He was being rude. But then again, so was she.

"You'll never be ready for this. This"—he rubbed her belly—"will never come at a time that works for you, because your life revolves around work. And that's okay. It's who you are. But adjustments have to be made on both sides. Now that we're going to have a baby, we need to realize we're not just living for ourselves anymore." The realization hurt as it hit him. What he wanted, what he longed for, dreamed for, didn't matter anymore. Sure, for one brief moment he thought he could make things work—his home life and work life. But not the way he wanted. Not with him being halfway across the world.

"I'm trying, Brian. I really am."

He reached for her hand and held it, his thumb lazily stroking her skin.

She was trying. He was being too hard on her and it wasn't fair. He noticed a bunch of pamphlets on the coffee table. He picked one up and turned the pages. There was lots of information on preeclampsia and how to handle the stress of bed rest.

"What's this?" He held out a pamphlet with the image of a baby with the title "Reborn" on it.

Diane reached for the paper and shook her head. "Just something Walter gave to me today."

"But what is it?" He vaguely recalled something about these dolls from reading it somewhere, or maybe it was on a television show. Dolls that looked lifelike.

"Reborn dolls. They're quite popular for those who collect dolls and such."

"But you don't." Diane with a doll? What was Walter thinking?

She rolled her eyes. "Of course I don't. This is a personal friend of Walter's. She has a unique way of making these dolls and works with different medical practices in the city whose patients suffer miscarriages or stillbirths."

"And he gave this to you why?" He went to grab the pamphlet out of her hand, but she caught his movement at the last second and held it out of his reach.

"She can create a doll from one of the 3-D ultrasounds I've had." Diane stared off into the distance as a soft smile appeared on her face. "I thought it was cute. The thought of holding our baby, even before he or she is born . . . I kind of like the idea."

"Seriously, Diane? That's the craziest thing I've heard." He shook his head in disgust.

She shrugged. "You're probably right. It seemed neat at the time, but . . . it is weird, isn't it?"

"Just a bit. What was Walter thinking? No"—he held up his hand—"don't answer that. The less I know about Walter's thought process the better. Hungry?"

"Starving." Her lips quirked as she rubbed her belly.

"Well, then, how about I take care of that for you." He pushed himself up from the couch, leaned down, and placed a gentle kiss on her forehead. "I'll do everything I can to make sure you and our baby are protected."

"That's what I'm worried about."

Brian pretended to ignore that as he walked out of the room.

———

Brian relaxed on their bed while Diane enjoyed her nightly bath. A golf tournament played on the television, but he barely paid attention to it. Instead, he wrote a list of pros and cons on a sheet of paper, unsure whether he really wanted to mention his recent job offer to Diane or whether he should quietly decline without her knowing about it.

How could he leave her now, especially at a time like this?

He wrote the word *preeclampsia* down on the con side and made a mental note to look into it more when he was alone, so he knew exactly what was happening.

"How did your meeting go after work?" Diane called out from the bathroom.

Brian pursed his lips and flicked the pen across the room.

"It was okay. Nothing too exciting."

He expected her to believe him. His meetings were nothing like hers and she rarely showed too much interest unless he needed her to. He glanced down at his sheet and realized the list of cons was longer than the pros. The only words he had on the pro side of the sheet were *goals, travel, promotion*, and *I want to*.

I want to. Bottom line, that was the real reason he wanted to take the offered position. President of international operations and communication. President. He'd never expected to have that title unless he opened his own firm, something he'd toyed with early in his career, before he realized it was easier to let someone else worry about the details while he played with the software.

Every word on the con side had to do with Diane and the baby. Not that his family was a con, just that it was a valid reason for not taking the position. Even if the idea of saying no, when he knew Diane would say yes if she'd been the one offered the position, irked him.

This was not a case of *if the shoe were on the other foot*, though. He couldn't think that way. It wasn't fair, not to him and not to Diane.

"Really? Did Tim just want to have a beer to celebrate the week or was it for something else?"

There was a splashing sound before the plug was pulled and water swished down the drain. Brian got up from the bed and went to help Diane out of the bath.

"Who all was there? Just the two of you?" Diane asked as Brian reached for her hands and pulled her to her feet.

He could tell she was fishing. It probably didn't help that all through dinner he tried to direct the conversation away from him and onto her. He should have known it wouldn't have worked.

"No, the big boss and the witch were there."

"Esther?" Her eyebrows rose as she wrapped a towel around her body.

He nodded.

"You didn't get fired, did you?"

Brian smiled at the half laugh in Diane's voice.

"That's what I thought too. Turned out to be the opposite."

He turned and headed back into their bedroom, flopping back down on the bed. Diane walked over to the little sitting area where she kept a basket of lotions and started to slather some on her body. Brian watched her closely, enjoying the small movements of her hands as she rubbed the cream onto her legs and arms.

"A promotion?"

"Of sorts."

Diane stilled and glanced up. He could read the expression on her face and knew she was trying to figure out what promotion he would have received and why he wasn't excited about it.

"You need to travel more, don't you?"

He nodded. She was smart, that woman of his.

"How much?"

Brian grabbed the remote and flicked through some random channels.

"Doesn't really matter. I'm not taking it." He tried to make it sound casual, as if he didn't care. But his voice croaked at the last minute.

"Why not?" She crossed the room and sat down on the bed beside him.

He just stared at her but didn't respond. She'd figure it out.

"What was the position?" She reached for his hand and threaded her fingers through his.

"President of international operations and communication." He kept his eyes glued to the television, not willing to see the pity in her eyes. He knew she knew he was turning it down for her. Knowing they both knew it was enough.

"President of international operations and communication," Diane quietly repeated, letting it sink in. "That's wonderful! How can you turn that down?"

Brian sighed.

"International operations, Diane. They want me stationed out of London. I told them I couldn't. You have your job and we have our baby. Moving halfway across the world isn't something that would work for us right now." His chest suddenly tightened. For some insane reason, he felt like he was going to cry. Talking about it with Diane made it real.

Diane reached for the remote, tossed it to the side, and forced him to focus on her.

"We will make it work. You can't turn this down. Not now. Brian, this is what you've always wanted." She stared him in the eyes, suddenly serious. "We can make it work," she repeated.

Brian shook his head. No, they couldn't. Sure, he'd admit he held on to a smidgen of hope that she would say "go for it," but not now. Not when she was bedridden.

"How? It's not possible. You can't travel, not now, and there's no way I'm leaving you alone. And what about your job, your promotion, the one you've worked so hard for? You can't give that up."

Diane pursed her lips. "Please tell me you haven't said no yet."

"I haven't said no. Yet."

She smiled, as if she had all the answers to all their problems. "We talked about getting a nanny, right? Well, let's hire one sooner. She can help me while I'm on bed rest and you can go and check out this position and what it all means. I have time off after the baby comes, so we can go on an extended vacation and stay with you in London. Whether we raise the baby here or there doesn't matter, not in the beginning. We'll take one day at a time. I told you not to stop traveling, didn't I? We will make this work."

The pressure that had been growing in Brian's chest all evening lifted with her words. They would make this work. He knew it. They could do it. They would do it.

He couldn't say anything. All he did was smile before leaning forward and showing his wife just how much he loved her with a passionate kiss.

CHAPTER TWENTY-TWO

Diane

Present–July

I locked myself in my room. I haven't wanted to see anyone for a few days now, but Nina wouldn't listen. Now she would. The door was locked.

Grace cried in her bassinet. She'd been crying for the past hour or more and I'd never felt so hopeless in my life.

I listened as I rocked myself on my bed, but I couldn't go to her. Instead, I just covered my ears with my hands. Her cries hurt me, they hurt my ears, they hurt my head, they hurt my heart. Nothing I did soothed her. I held her, I rocked her, I tried to feed her. But it didn't matter. I wasn't what she needed.

"Shhh, sweet baby. Shhh." I knew she couldn't hear me over her cries, but it was all I could do. Every tear, sob, and scream ripped me apart but I was helpless. What kind of mother was I when I couldn't even calm my own child down?

A horrible one. Rotten. Selfish.

Why did I think I could do this? Why did I ever think that I could raise a child on my own? I couldn't. I should never have even tried. I knew. I knew back when I first found out I was pregnant that I couldn't do this. I'd never had those motherly instincts everyone mentioned. I'd never even wanted a child.

Charlie was right. She'd been right all along. I needed to tell her. I had to tell her. She could never have a baby. Ever.

"I can't do this. I can't do this. I can't do this," I chanted over and over and over again. I needed to block out Grace's cries before I went crazy.

I grabbed the journal and pen off the side table by my bed and flipped to an empty page. Except there was none. How could there not be an empty page? There had to be. I had to write. I had something important to say and I needed to get it out before I forgot. Again.

I shook the book upside down and a piece of folded paper fluttered down to my lap, dancing as it made its way down, like a lazy butterfly looking for a perch. I blew a soft breath toward it, to see it dance some more, but it'd already landed.

I plucked the paper from my lap and opened it. A smile slid across my lips, pulling the edges until I felt like a marionette. All I needed were the strings and I'd be free to dance to someone else's tune.

The words I needed to write, the ones that played over and over in my head, were already written down on this paper. This was perfect.

"Shhh, baby. It's all going to be okay now." I crawled across the bed to where the bassinet lay and watched my angel as tears gathered in her eyes and her cries grew louder. I knew she was trying to tell me something but I couldn't understand it. But I would. I knew I could if I could just listen to her.

I reached down and slid my arms beneath her wriggling body and brought her close to my chest. I knew what I had to do. It was the same thing my mother had to do. I understood it now. It all made sense.

She did love us more than life. And she proved that to us. She made the ultimate sacrifice to ensure our happiness, our well-being, and our safety.

All I wanted in life was to be like her.

I wiped the small drops of tears on Grace's face with the pad of my thumb.

"Shhh, baby. It's all going to be okay now. Trust me. I know what to do. I understand it now."

I held Grace tight to my chest and listened as her cries softened. I stared down at the note in front of me and the image of my mother filled my mind. She was so beautiful with her soft brown hair gathered in a braid down her back and the twinkle in her eyes as she smiled down at me. I imagined the feel of her lips as she laid that last kiss on my forehead.

I love you more than life, she'd whispered to me.

The words she'd written on her note became clear. Clearer than anything else in my life.

There is nothing I want more in life than to be a mother.

There's no greater gift.

Laying my life down with gladness in my heart and a smile on my face is an honor, a gift to those I love.

My children will know that I sacrificed all for their happiness.

Hush now. Your tears rip me in half. Just close your eyes and let go. All will be well when we open our eyes once again.

Then we'll be together in a world where there will be no more tears.

I love you more than life.

CHAPTER TWENTY-THREE

Brian

November 2013

All was quiet in the house as Brian sipped his morning coffee and stared out into their backyard. There wasn't much time left before he needed to leave, but everything was packed and all he had to do was grab his messenger bag with his laptop.

He couldn't believe he was doing this. He loved this house. Loved every nook and cranny and had created fantasies about their life here, about making this house a home. And yet here he was, leaving to find another place in London. A place where he would live alone until Diane could join him. He knew it would be nothing compared to what they had here.

Was he doing the right thing? There was a part of him that wasn't sure. This, today, leaving here, seemed to be final. He didn't like it.

"Good morning, Mr. Wright."

Brian shook his head. The woman they'd hired to help Diane while he was away, who would hopefully continue on as their nanny, refused to call him by his first name. He wasn't sure why.

"Nina, please, call me Brian." He turned and watched as she chose fresh fruit from a bowl on the kitchen island and washed it.

"Would you like some fruit? I'd be more than happy to slice up extra."

Brian shook his head. He'd eat on the plane. It was more important to him that Diane eat something. In the past month, he'd watched her belly grow larger while the rest of her grew smaller, if that was even possible. She refused to eat much, complaining that lying in a bed or sitting in a chair really didn't demand much sustenance. Not being physically active was getting to her. Lately, all she ate was fruit and vegetables with the occasional piece of sliced chicken. No pasta, no desserts.

Normally he'd be worried, but Nina was also a nurse. He felt comfortable knowing Diane was in her care.

"I can't thank you enough—"

"No need."

Brian refilled his cup. "No, there is a need. I can't thank you enough for doing this for us, for coming on board and helping us the way you have. I know it's . . . not the pace you're used to, but knowing you're here, taking care of Diane and our baby while I'll be away, means more to me than I can ever express."

Her credentials were superb, and he'd been quite surprised when she arrived at their house for their first interview. She's come recommended by their doctor, who had worked with Nina for years. She'd specialized in pediatrics, had worked with the hospital in their crisis department for women who suffered from postpartum and other mental illnesses, and also had experience in the private sector. He knew that no matter what occurred, she'd be able to support Diane. God knew he wouldn't be able to. He couldn't help but think Nina coming along was an answer to a prayer. If anything . . . as much as he hated to even think it . . . but if there were any issues, like with Diane's mother, at least Nina would be there.

"I'm doing what I love, and the slower pace is nice after all my years in the field. Don't worry, Mr. . . . Brian. I'm not going anywhere. I'm here for as long as you and your wife need me."

He breathed a sigh of relief.

"Even if it means coming to London?" He'd mentioned it to her last week, coming with Diane and the baby if Diane needed the help.

He knew nanny duty wasn't really in her portfolio, but he'd watched how close the two women had become lately and he hated the thought of having to find someone else. She asked for time to consider the request last week and he'd been waiting ever since. Just in case the answer was no, he had contacted a local agency.

"Yes. I would like to continue on as your nanny while in London for the first few months. Not as a permanent position, but I would be more than happy to help in finding a replacement once Diane is comfortable." She'd finished slicing the fruit and arranged it all on a plate. She prepared a tray to take to Diane.

"Wonderful. Thank you. We'll take whatever time you can give us." He poured himself a new cup of coffee and placed it on the tray. "Here, let me take that." He reached for it. "I'll sit with Diane for a bit before I need to leave."

"She's going to miss you. She tries to hide it, but your leaving is hard on her."

Nina's words stopped Brian. He set the tray back down and stared at her, trying to read the expression on her face. Worry. Fear. Anxiety. That was what he saw and it chilled him.

"What do you mean? Why are you telling me this now, right before I leave?"

Nina poured herself a cup of coffee before sitting down at the breakfast nook in front of the window. Brian joined her when she made it clear she wasn't going to say anything more until he sat with her.

"She's worried she can't do this alone."

"She's not alone." That didn't make sense to him.

"She will be once you leave."

"You're here. Which is almost better than if I were, since you'll know what to do if anything goes . . . wrong." Even thinking that something could go wrong churned his stomach. "And I'll be back before her due date. She knows this."

Nina's lips pursed as she took a sip of her coffee. "We both know that knowing something and believing in it are two different things.

She's afraid but she doesn't want you to see that. These next few days, after you leave, will be the worst for her."

It was as if Nina spoke another language. Nothing made sense. Diane wasn't afraid. He'd never seen her so at peace. Okay, so she didn't like being housebound, but the tension she always carried was gone. Her workload was cut in half and she appeared to accept her own limitations. She even seemed happy. At least, she did when they were together.

"Are you sure?"

Nina nodded.

"Should I stay home then? Not go? What are you trying to tell me?"

"I'm only trying to show you what your wife is trying to hide. So you can be aware."

Brian rubbed at his face and noticed the time on his watch.

"I need to go soon. Please send me updates through e-mail on how she is and if I need to come home, okay?" He reached across and grabbed the woman's hand. "Keep her safe. Please. She's all that matters to me, more than this job, more than anything else."

He watched her face to see if she would tell him the truth or just placate him. A seed of fear settled deep inside of him.

"She's the one you should be telling that to."

"I will. Please let me know when my taxi arrives." He gathered the tray in his hands and headed toward the stairs. He would tell Diane. He'd make sure he showed her too, every single day he was away. He wouldn't let a day go by that he didn't show her just how much he loved her. One way or another.

"She wants to drive you to the airport herself."

He stopped and glanced over his shoulder. "She can't. Can she?"

Nina shrugged. "She shouldn't, but she won't listen to me."

"Then she'll just need to listen to me." He gave Nina a small smile before continuing his way toward the stairs.

They'd say their good-byes here, at home, where he knew she and their unborn baby were okay.

―――

"Don't look at me like that," Brian pleaded as he paced back and forth in their bedroom.

Diane sat at her desk and sipped at her coffee. She'd gotten dressed while he'd been downstairs and now picked at her breakfast while he tried to convince her to stay home.

"Then stop being so unreasonable." She speared a strawberry and waved it at him.

Unreasonable? He was being unreasonable? She was the one on bed rest.

"We can say good-bye here. It's only a ten-minute drive to the airport. I've already called for a taxi." He gripped the top of a chair opposite her desk and tried to smile. He felt sick to his stomach and he wasn't sure why.

"Exactly. It's only a ten-minute drive. It's not going to hurt me or the baby. Would you relax, please?!"

"Diane . . ." He stopped when he caught the tear in her eye. That was it. He was done for. Why even bother arguing when it meant so much to her? She'd be fine. Ever since they got the news of the pre-eclampsia, Diane had kept herself on a strict regimen of staying in bed at all times unless absolutely necessary.

He moved to be beside her, squatted down, and took her hands into his own. "I love you, and leaving you here, now, is the hardest thing I've ever had to do." He was going to say no; he had to say no. Her health and the welfare of their baby were more important than her seeing him off. He was about to say that when he caught the shimmer of tears in her eyes. "Ah, hell. If your coming means I get to spend ten more minutes with you, then I will cherish those minutes every moment I'm away." He leaned forward and placed a kiss on her protruding belly. "I'm going to miss you too, little one," he whispered.

Her fingers wove through his hair in response. He stood up, bringing her with him, and folded his arms around her. This was where he belonged, with her, in his arms. Nothing else felt more right.

"I am going to be fine. We're going to be fine. And you're only going to be gone for a few weeks, so nothing to get all worked up over, right?" Her voice, muffled against his shirt, didn't mask the sob she was trying to stop.

Brian tightened his hold, wishing he could imprint the feel of his arms around her on himself. He didn't like the tears. Didn't like knowing this was so hard on her.

"Hey." He pulled back, just a little, so he could look down at her. "I'll be back before you know it. I'll find us the perfect place and get the office on schedule, then be back here with plenty of time to pamper you before our baby is due. I promise."

She nodded.

"And good news: Nina said she'll stay on after the baby is born."

A small smile spread across Diane's lips. "I know. She told me this morning. I think it had something to do with wanting to see Europe for the first time."

"I'll take whatever we can get from her." Brian was just happy she was staying on. They'd work on the timing later. He'd figure out a way to get her to stay with them permanently if that was what Diane wanted and needed.

"Think we could stop for a coffee and a muffin on our way?" Diane stepped out of his embrace and reached for her purse on her desk.

Brian tried to not act surprised. A muffin? He'd buy her a dozen if she wanted. Anything to get her to eat.

He caught the glint of gold around her neck and pulled at the necklace hidden beneath the neckline of her shirt.

Diane blushed as she held up her hand. That was when he noticed her finger was ringless.

"They won't fit due to the swelling, but I didn't want to put them in the jewelry box. Nina was the one to suggest wearing them around my neck. I didn't want to take them off but they were cutting off circulation in my finger."

Brian kissed the swollen finger where her rings once were. Why hadn't he noticed this before now? He understood why she had to take them off, but he'd be lying if he didn't admit seeing her finger bare bothered him.

"Just a little bit longer." He gave her a kiss before leading her out of the room and down the stairs.

Nina stood at the door. "I'll take care of the taxi."

"We're going to stop for coffee and muffins. I'll bring you back one." Diane beamed a smile as she linked her arm through Brian's.

Brian caught the bemused look on Nina's face.

"As long as it's chocolate and you'll have one too, that would be lovely."

"Oh, I think today is a chocolate kind of day." A cloud passed over Diane's face for a moment.

Brian thought about the small box full of cards, letters, and word games he'd made for Diane to enjoy while he was gone. He'd given it to Nina last night, asking her to give Diane one a day. There should be enough in there to last until he came home. It was a small way to show her how much he loved and missed her. He knew it was sentimental and might seem cheesy, but he hoped she liked it.

Brian linked his fingers through Diane's as he carried her to the SUV. She'd made a fuss about it when he lifted her up in his arms, but he'd told her to hush. He couldn't believe how light she felt. The worry niggled at him while he made sure she was buckled in before getting his suitcases and messenger bag from the hallway.

"She's way too light, Nina. I don't like it. Try to get her to eat more while I'm gone, will you? I need you to take good care of her." He placed his hand on Nina's shoulder as she waited at the door.

"She's in your care right now. That's all you need to worry about. Go on before you miss your flight and we have to do this all over again.

I'll follow you after the taxi gets here. Tell her to wait for me at the airport and I'll drive her home. Just don't tell her until you get there."

A sense of relief washed over him as he looked at this older woman who had become their lifesaver. What would they do without her when she decided to leave them?

"Thank you. I feel better knowing you'll be there to drive her home. I don't want anything to happen to her or our baby." He reached out and gave Nina a hug, a move that surprised both of them.

"Go on now." She pushed him away before closing the door behind him.

Brian stopped midway down the stone path and turned in a slow circle, wanting to take in every detail of his house and yard. It amazed him how much he loved this place, how at peace he felt every time he turned the corner onto their street and their home came into view. This was where he belonged and where he wanted to be. Knowing this, realizing it at the very minute he was leaving, hurt. Whatever place he found in London would only be temporary. It might mean more traveling, but he'd make it work. He had to. He knew that once Diane's maternity leave was up, she'd be ready to get back to work, and that work wasn't overseas.

The tightness in his chest didn't abate as he pulled out of his driveway. He rolled his shoulders to relieve some tension and winced at the loud crack from his neck.

"You forgot to book an appointment with your chiropractor, didn't you?" Diane shook her head before reaching for his hand.

"There wasn't enough time."

She pulled out her phone. "I'll make a note to schedule one for when you return, okay?"

"Thanks, babe." Brian smiled as he slowed down as the light ahead turned red.

"I know it's only for two weeks, but I'll do my best to see if I can make it home sooner."

Diane squeezed his hand. "Would you stop worrying? We've gone longer. Remember that time in Dubai when you were gone for almost four months? This is nothing. If the baby decides to come sooner than expected, I'll let you know. I promise. Besides, it's not like I'm alone. I have Nina."

The light was still red. He turned slightly in his seat. "The first twinge of a contraction, you let me know, okay?" He was serious, but he couldn't stop the smile from spreading as Diane chuckled. It was less than half a day to London. That should be more than enough time for him to hop on a plane and make it to the hospital if she went into labor. From what he'd read, first births always took longer than expected. He hoped that was true in this case.

"Promise. As long as Junior here behaves, you'll already be home. Oh, do me a favor?"

Brian's finger tapped on the steering wheel as he waited for the light to turn green. The clock was ticking and he'd promised they'd stop for coffee still. Thankfully, there was a coffee shop with a drive-thru close to the airport.

"What's that?" He leaned over and placed a small kiss on her cheek. He'd do anything for her. Anything.

"Bring me home some macarons from Ladurée? It's in Harrods." The little wink she gave him had him chuckling.

"You're kidding me?" He shook his head in mock exasperation. "You want me to go to Harrods? That place is a maze!"

The light turned green and Brian stepped on the gas.

"Please?" Diane squeezed his hand again before her grip tightened and her eyes widened in fear.

Time slowed as Brian turned his attention from his wife to what she was staring at. As he turned his head, the images in front of him were burned in his mind. The shopkeeper bent over a sign he was fixing to the ground, an elderly lady yanking her dog back from crossing the street, the multitude of flowers outside a florist's shop. Time stood still as he fixated on all those small images before looking out his driver window and realizing none of it mattered.

Headlights from an oncoming truck faced him, blinding him as Diane's horrific screams filled the vehicle.

Brian leaned forward and toward Diane. He knew they were about to get hit and he wanted to keep her out of the way. He grabbed her hand just as the other vehicle ran through the red light and smashed into their SUV. The impact of metal upon metal grated in his ears as he was flung about. His chest dug into the gearshift as his door buckled and pushed against him.

The image of Diane hunched over, trying to protect her belly, was the last thing he saw before it all went black.

———

A loud roar startled him. He tried to open his eyes but he couldn't. It was as if they were glued shut. His head hung at an awkward angle and he struggled to lift it, to ease the sharp pain that ran through his body, but even that proved to be too difficult.

Someone spoke to him, but it sounded was like he was underwater; the words were muffled and at too far a distance for him to make out. Things prodded at him, moved him, and the pain that seemed to settle over him like a wet blanket now pierced one location, his head. It was going to explode. Whatever was happening to him, it had to stop. Now.

He tried to tell them, to beg them to leave him be, that he needed the pain to stop, but when he opened his mouth, all he could do was moan.

"Just relax; we have you."

Fingers prodded at his eyes, forcing them apart, and he caught sight of a hand, a small light flashing in front of his face, and then other faces before him as he struggled to figure out where he was.

Diane! Where was his wife? Brian needed to move, to see where he was, to find Diane, but he couldn't lift his arms, his head, or any other part of his body.

"Diane. Where is she? Where's my wife? Where is she?" His voice cracked with each word he forced out.

"Calm down. Please, sir, calm down. I need you to lie still. We're attempting to get her out of the vehicle now. We've got her; don't worry." The voice was calm, in control. Brian trusted the voice. He had to.

A heavy weight settled over him, compressing him until he was sure his body was crushing under the weight. The pain was intolerable but it hurt too much to cry. His head was going to explode any moment; he knew it.

"She's pregnant. Please, please be careful. She's pregnant. Please . . ." It was getting too hard to talk. All he wanted to do was stop, to be still, to let the pain wash over him until it carried him away. It would be easier that way.

"We've got her. It'll be okay. You can relax now. She's safe." There was a slight edge to the voice now.

Brian wanted to ask what was wrong. He could tell. He knew it from the way the person spoke. Diane was in trouble. She couldn't be. No, she couldn't be. He should have made her stay at home, should have listened to himself.

This was all his fault. That was the last thing he thought, a mantra that repeated over and over before he couldn't think anymore.

CHAPTER TWENTY-FOUR

Diane

Present—August

The remnants of a beautiful dream drifted away from me. The sweet smile Grace would give me as she looked up at me, the way her eyes lit up as I tickled her toes. The happiness that overwhelmed me and made everything right in my world. I dreamed of Brian and the way he'd hold me close when he knew I needed a hug. I could still feel his arms around me.

I wanted to hold on those feelings, to keep them close. I rolled over and reached my hand out to where Grace's bassinet lay, but nothing was there. I cracked open my eyes and saw a bare floor where there should have been a chair that held the bassinet. My hand dropped as a crushing weight rested on my chest. For some reason, deep inside, I knew the bassinet wouldn't be there.

"Nina?" I called out. I rose up and rested on my elbow and was about to call again when I noticed my room.

It was different. Gone were my cream walls and large space, my sitting area and desk and large en suite. Gone.

I shot up out of bed and flung my legs over. My feet hit the edge of a worn floor mat.

"Nina?" I couldn't keep the panic out of my voice. The white walls, the bare floor, even the thin blanket I'd just shoved aside, all looked like something you'd find in a hospital.

What happened to me? Why was I here?

"Nina!" My fingers clutched the edge of the mattress as I screamed. My body froze and my muscles tightened as I continued to call out Nina's name. My eyes were glued to the door. I waited for the knob to turn, for the slash of light that sneaked in under the door to alter, but there was nothing. Nothing. No one answered. No one heard my screams.

I was all alone. A vise gripped my heart and squeezed. I was all alone.

I slipped my feet into the slippers that were on the mat and ran over to the door and turned the knob.

"Nina. Somebody. Anyone hear me?" I opened the door, not sure what I expected, but seeing a bare wall with a single metal chair directly opposite my door wasn't it.

I stepped into the hallway but kept my hand on the door knob. "Please. Somebody help me." All the energy in me evaporated at the stillness around me. Where was I? "Please. Someone, anybody, please . . ."

There was a door at the end of the hall, the type of cold, metal door you'd expect to find in any type of hospital. At the other end were a few doors and as I continued to yell out, one of those doors opened.

"What's with all the racket? Simmer down, Diane, before they do it for you." Some strange woman held up her finger against her lips and hushed me.

"Help me, please?" I asked her. I had no idea who she was, but that didn't matter. I was desperate.

"What's your problem this morning? Go back to bed. You know Nina will be here soon."

My knees buckled and my legs folded as I collapsed onto the cold hard floor. I had no idea what was going on. I swiped at the tears on my face and struggled to my feet. There had to be an answer somewhere in this room. Maybe I was sick. Maybe I'd been in an acc . . . oh God, no. No, no, no.

I pushed myself up and stumbled back into my room and made my way toward the small bathroom. There was a heavy haze in my mind as I splashed water on my face and looked up in horror. I barely recognized myself. My eyes were bloodshot and haggard, and the lines around them as well as on my forehead were more noticeable than before. I had to be dreaming. That was it. There was no other explanation. I just needed to wake myself up.

Please, God, let me wake up.

There was a window in my room with blinds over the glass panes. At the top was a knob. I turned it and the world outside opened up and the sunshine filtered into the room. Directly across from me was a park full of large trees and walkways lined with flowerbeds. Below me were benches but there was no one outside. I recognized the pathway below, the benches, even the park. I had been there before. Snapshots of sitting on the bench flashed through my mind, then flittered away before I could grab onto them.

Where was I? I didn't recognize the building I was in. From my angle I counted four floors beneath me, and who knew if there were any above me.

There wasn't much to this room I was sequestered in. A bed. A rug. A small desk and chair, with a book on top along with a box wrapped with a fabric ribbon. I shrugged into the housecoat that lay across the foot of the bed and sat down at the desk. I touched the box and wondered what was in it. I lifted it up and it was lightweight.

About to untie the ribbon, I caught sight of the book and had to double-check the words written on it. *Diane's Memory Journal*. What?

I dropped the box and went to reach for the journal, when there was a slight knock on the door. I shot up from my chair and tugged the housecoat I wore tight around my waist.

"Diane?"

I sagged with relief when I heard Nina's voice. The moment she entered the room I rushed over and engulfed her in a large hug.

"Nina, I've been so scared. Where am I? Why am I here?" I gripped her shoulders and stared into her eyes.

There was a look there. A look of surprise and . . . relief? Why would she be relieved? She shook her head and a wall came between us as I continued to stare at her. I recognized that look. She'd put on her mask.

"How are you feeling today?" Nina placed her hands over mine and forced me to release her shoulders.

"I don't want to be here. Please, can we just go home?" I glanced around her to the barely opened door but she stepped back and closed it so I couldn't see out.

"Nina?" There was a look on her face, a look that told me too much but gave away nothing at the same time.

"Any headaches today, Diane?" Nina led me over to the bed and had me sit down. She sat beside me and folded her hands in her lap.

I stood back up. I didn't want to sit down. I couldn't sit down. Something was wrong.

"No." I shook my head. "For the first time in a long time, there's no headache. But what's going on, Nina?" I paced back and forth in the small room; the sound of my slippers as they shuffled along the floor was prominent in the silence.

"Do you know what day this is?" Nina pulled out the small notebook she carried with her all the time and opened it up.

"Day? I don't know." Honestly, why was the date important? "Summer sometime, by the looks of it." I stood at the window and glanced out at the flowers below.

"Do you remember anything from yesterday?"

I studied Nina as she wrote in her little notepad. What did she write in there every morning?

"Where's the tea?" She always came into my room with a tray carrying tea, some breakfast, and pills. Always.

"Tea? We'll have it when we go for breakfast, just like every other morning." She glanced up at me with a question in her eyes.

"You usually bring it in to me and we have breakfast together." I hugged myself tight.

Nina shook her head.

A tidal wave of fear swept through me as I tightened my arms around me. I knew in that moment that the nightmare I'd held at bay for so many years was no longer something I only dreamed about. It was now real.

My mother—

"Stop. Whatever you are thinking, just stop." Nina patted the bed. I bit my lip before I sank down beside her.

"Diane, you're in the hospital." She reached for my hands.

"Why?" My mind blanked and I couldn't think.

I read the pity in Nina's eyes and I wanted to cringe.

"You've been here since just after Christmas." I sat back in shock. What? How was that possible? I was home yesterday with Grace.

Nina shook her head. I must have said that out loud.

"You were here yesterday. And the day before that. And—"

I held my hand up and cut her off. I didn't want to hear it. She was lying. She had to be.

"Where's Grace?" The sudden urge to hold my daughter, to see her face, hit me hard.

She leaned forward and I scooted backward until my back was against the cold wall. I hugged my knees to my chest and rocked back and forth. This didn't make sense. None of this made sense. I shouldn't be here, not in this room. I should be at home, with my daughter, filling out her baby book, taking pictures of her . . .

"Where is my daughter?"

"Diane, Grace is . . ." She sighed. "Grace is dead."

I shook my head. "No. No. Don't you tell me she is dead. She's not. She can't be. I can feel her"—I hit my chest with the palm of my hand—"in here. I can feel her, Nina. She's not dead. She can't be." I covered my ears with my hands and dropped my chin onto my knees, blinking away the tears in my eyes. Then I remembered her cries and how I tried to calm her . . .

I raised my head and stared at Nina. "I didn't . . . please, God, please tell me I didn't . . ."

"No, no, of course you didn't." Nina touched me and I jumped. I pushed myself up from the bed and vaulted until I was over at the door. I pounded on it, screaming for help, for someone to come and open the door. Nina just sat there on the bed and waited until I stopped. I turned toward her and felt myself slipping, falling down to the floor.

Nina caught me in time and pulled me close, her arms wrapped around my body as I shook.

"Come sit down." Nina helped me to sit on the chair at the desk. She smoothed my hair back while I just stared at her, as if frozen.

I didn't know what to think. What to feel. What to say. I felt so lost and alone. So very, very alone.

Nina slumped against the wall by the window and glanced out. "Do you remember when Brian left to go to London?" She didn't look at me as she asked the question. But I caught the way her body stiffened ever so slightly.

"I do. I drove him." Why bring Brian into this? Unless he was the one who put me here and he now had Grace. Oh my God. That was it.

"Did Brian take her? Is that it?" A mixture of fear and relief overwhelmed me in that moment. Grace wasn't dead, thank God.

"No, Diane." She took a breath and let it out, the sigh deflating her body before she turned toward me. "Do you remember anything that happened after you left to take Brian to the airport?"

I nodded. "Of course. I came home. You were waiting for me by the front door and we ended up watching a movie together."

Nina shook her head. "No, honey, that's not what happened. You never made it home, Diane. On the way to the airport, a truck lost control of its brakes and ran through a red light, hitting your vehicle on the driver's side."

"Brian was driving," I whispered.

Nina nodded. "The ambulance was on the scene fairly quickly, but Brian died on the way to the hospital and you went into labor."

"Grace?" *Please, please don't say the words. Please don't say the words.*

Nina swallowed.

"She didn't survive?" I wanted to crumble, to fall, and never to get up again. I didn't want to hear this. I couldn't. I wasn't strong enough. That's why I was here, wasn't it? I wasn't strong enough. I stumbled to the chair and sat down, never once taking my eyes off Nina.

"She was stillborn. The impact . . . it was too much. It was my fault. I shouldn't have let you go." Nina turned back toward the window but her body shook almost as much as mine did at that moment.

Why couldn't I remember this?

"Was I in a coma?"

"No. God no. You were okay. " She wiped at the tears on her face and left her post at the wall to sit back on my bed.

"Then why don't I remember this? It's not true. It can't be. I held Grace in my arms. I remember her. God, Nina, I remember my daughter. I held her yesterday. She smiled at me." I banged my fist on the desk and the small box I'd looked at earlier flipped and fell over the side of the desk and onto the floor. For a moment, both Nina and I stared at it until I picked it up and held it in my lap.

"What's this?"

"Open it," Nina whispered.

I watched her as I slowly untied the ribbon. I popped open the lid and inside were two rings. Brian's wedding ring and mine. I lifted them out and slid them down my ring finger, but I couldn't get my own ring to move past my knuckle.

"The medication you're on makes your fingers swell." Nina winced as I took the ring off and placed it back in the box. I didn't want to think about the rings and what they meant. Not yet.

"Why does Grace seem so real to me then?"

Nina's hands knotted together as she glanced everywhere but at me.

"Do you recall a pamphlet you filled out and gave to Walter about Reborn dolls?"

I gave my head a quick shake but then gasped. I remembered. I remembered Brian thought it was creepy when I mentioned it to him and so I didn't tell him I'd given Walter a copy of our 3-D ultrasound. Walter wanted to get me a doll as a gift. Something we could keep for our child. And if we had a little girl, she could play with the doll as she grew. I didn't like the idea; I actually agreed with Brian that it was creepy, but this was a close friend of Walter's who was trying to get her business going, so as a favor, I said yes.

"I made Walter cancel the order, though, after Brian said he didn't like the idea."

Nina shrugged. "Walter forgot. Around Christmas, a package arrived at the door. I had gone out to run some errands; otherwise I would have caught the delivery and maybe none of this would have happened." Defeat washed over her as she finally looked up at me.

I knew right away she blamed herself for all of this. Whatever all of this was.

"So Walter didn't . . . come to the house and leave the box?" I remembered that or at least, I thought I did. When Nina pursed her lips together I knew that's not how it happened.

She leaned forward and clasped her hands over her knees. "You opened the box and inside was a tiny baby, the same size Grace would have been. It was too much for you to process. When I came home, you were up in the nursery rocking the doll as if it were real."

No. No, she was wrong. I would have known that it was only a doll. Maybe she'd caught me at a weak moment. That was all.

"Grace isn't alive?" My world splintered apart. I could feel the cracks as they happened in my heart, the way they ripped me apart one at a time.

"No, honey. She's not."

"And Brian's not in London? He didn't leave me?"

Nina blinked but didn't respond.

"All those letters from him that you'd give me in the mornings . . . they were real, right?" I needed to know that I didn't make those up. *Please say they were real.*

"They're all right here." Diane reached for a shoebox beneath my bed.

I reached for it, opened the lid, and sighed with relief to find a little bit of reality inside this box. Memories I won't need to worry were real or not. I saw a little Post-it note that said *I love you* and swallowed back a lump in my throat.

"Was anything else real? Our morning teas and sitting outside in the backyard? Going into work? What about the baby book I've been working on? And Charlie? Where is my sister?" I squeezed the bridge of my nose as I clenched my eyes closed. My head throbbed from the pressure.

Nina's touch on my knee startled me. She knelt in front of me, tears in her eyes. "As soon as she could, Charlie came home. She's been here every day to sit with you."

"Where is she then?" I didn't know what to believe.

"She'll be here shortly. Marcus met her in Texas and they both flew in this morning. She'll be here soon." Nina's shoulders dropped. "I'm so sorry, Diane. I'm so sorry."

I glanced around the room we were in and saw it clearly. The simple bed with a small rug for my cold feet in the morning. The bedside table with no adornments. The four white walls that were bare and cold.

"I've gone crazy, haven't I?"

Nina's eyes closed. She bowed her head but I heard the words. I would never forget them.

Yes.

"I'm just like my mother. Aren't I?"

Nina nodded. "You have postpartum psychosis."

That was all I needed to hear. I was crazy.

"You're not crazy. You have a hormonal imbalance that was triggered by traumatic events your brain couldn't handle properly."

Traumatic events. I could still hear Grace's laughter; I could see her smile. I could feel Brian's arms around me as he held me close, the kiss he gave me when I dropped him off at the airport.

How could that not be real? How?

"I don't understand. It's all so real to me." My throat ached as I swallowed past the lump lodged there.

Nina reached for the journal on the desk.

"Every day you would write in this journal. Instead of dealing with your loss, your mind wanted to protect itself. So you retreated into a world where Grace was still alive. It's all here." She opened the book and flipped through the pages. She wore a sad smile as she read some of the words.

"Without fail, as soon as we had our tea in the morning, you would come back to your room, sit at this desk, and write in here. This was your way of keeping Grace real while learning to deal with Brian's loss."

"But I didn't know he was dead."

"No. But you knew he'd left you. This was just an easier way for you to handle the loss. For now."

She handed me the journal.

"Our minds are a mystery. We all handle tragedy differently. This has been hard on you. And it's a lot to process."

There was a soft knock on the door. Nina squeezed my shoulder as she went to answer it. I held the journal in my hands and felt like my whole world had just been destroyed in one swoop.

I recognized Charlie's voice on the other side of the door. So she was real. She was really here.

"Charlie?" I called out. As soon as my little sister rushed into the room with her arms out wide, I couldn't control myself any longer and my body doubled over with the weight of reality pressing down hard. I sobbed as she caught me and held me tight.

"It's okay, honey; it's okay. I promise. We'll get through this. I'm right here. You're not alone." Her soothing voice calmed me as she continued to hold me.

Nothing I knew was real. Nothing. I wasn't sure which was better: living in reality or living in a dreamworld I'd obviously created for myself.

Something told me the answer to that question lay in the journal I still held. I pulled away from her and wiped at my tears.

"It's all true then?"

No one said anything, but I knew, no matter how many times I asked the question, the answer would be the same. Always.

Brian was dead. Grace . . . I'd never hold Grace in my arms again. I wanted to crawl back under the thin covers and force myself to sleep. Maybe then I'd go back to the world where my baby was still alive.

I grabbed hold of Charlie's hand and squeezed. "This journal . . ." I didn't have the words to finish what I wanted to say, what I needed to ask.

Charlie knelt down in front of me. "Remember the journals we used to write in as kids when we first moved in with Aunt Mags? Think of this book like one of those journals. We used to make up stories about what life would be like if Mom had been around, remember? And then when you started talking again before me, you'd tell me stories about our parents—" Charlie's voice broke as she struggled to contain the tears I could see glimmering in her eyes.

I nodded my head, remembering that time. I used to make up stories for her, stories that hid the scars, the fears that kept her locked inside her head. Aunt Mags used to tell me I had a gift for words.

I wanted to fling the journal away from me. I couldn't imagine ever wanting to open it and read about the world I'd created for myself. A world based on a false reality.

"None of this is true then? Nothing in this book happened? It was all in my head?" I tried to wrap my head around that but couldn't. It would mean that I never sat with Grace outside; we never went on that walk where I lost control of her stroller; I never took pictures and sent them to Brian . . . oh God, Brian.

"Some of it was real. What you wrote about when I came home, that was real. Being outside, the walks we took . . . some of it was real." Charlie swallowed hard. I noticed her ring finger.

"What about Marcus? Was any of that real?"

A soft smile grew on Charlie's face. "That was real. And he's here. He flew in, since he knew I wasn't going to be returning to the camp for a while."

I nodded. At least she would have Marcus, while I had nothing but my memories. "My phone, where is my phone?" I took thousands of pictures of Grace. I know I did. If I could just see them, then maybe this was a nightmare and I'd wake up.

But I could tell by the slight shake of Nina's head that this was no nightmare.

"What am I supposed to do now?" I rubbed my forehead with my fingers, trying to dispel the dull thud of a headache forming. Nina must have caught my gesture as she placed her hand on Charlie's shoulder.

"Why don't we grab some breakfast?" Nina suggested. "This is a lot to process and we don't need to do it all at once."

Charlie nodded. "Maybe we could go for a walk outside? Try to clear our heads and take in the fresh air?"

I sat there, unsure of what to do or how to react. Pressure built up in my chest and there was nothing I wanted to do more than lie down. I shook my head and groaned as a wave of dizziness swept over me.

"I need a moment," I mumbled. I wasn't sure anyone heard me, since they were talking between themselves, so I pushed myself to my feet and took the necessary two steps to my bed.

"Diane?" Charlie pulled back the covers for me and I curled up on my side, clutching the journal tight to my chest. What I wanted was to hold my baby close, to breathe in that baby-fresh smell, but I couldn't. I would never be able to do that again.

"Did I even get to hold her?" I whispered.

Charlie sat down beside me. "You did, for a long time. She was so tiny and beautiful. You called her your angel."

My angel. I wished I could remember that.

"Brian? Did I say good-bye to him?"

"Oh, honey." Charlie's breath hitched. "You did. Walter arranged a memorial for him and you were there. You don't remember?"

I shook my head and fought against the swell of tears forming. I didn't want to cry. I refused to cry. Not now. Later, when I was alone and the whispers in my head were quieter.

"It's okay, Diane. Memory loss is normal after electroshock therapy," Nina said before she opened the door.

"Shock therapy?" I didn't even know how to process this. My body started to shake and Charlie reached for my hand.

"It's going to be okay, Dee. I promise. It's a good thing. It brought you back to us."

My eyes filled with tears as I tried to process everything. It brought me back, but to what? I'm all alone now. Without Brain, without Grace . . . who was I?

After Nina left the room, I sat up and scooted across the bed until my back was against the wall. I pulled the blanket over my legs and then leaned my head against Charlie's shoulder as she sat beside me.

"Will you help me know what was real and what wasn't?" I laid the journal in my lap, trying to find the courage I wasn't sure I had, and opened up to the first page.

"Of course I will," Charlie whispered to me.

CHAPTER TWENTY-FIVE

Diane

Six months later

I held a picture frame in my hand and glanced around the almost empty room. Six months had passed since that day in the hospital when I realized my world had turned upside down. Six long months of therapy, medication, and trying to sort reality from the dreamworld I still wished I lived in.

"Are you sure you don't want any help in here?" Nina stood at the bedroom door of what was supposed to have been Grace's baby room.

"No, I need to do this. You know that."

She gave me a sad smile before she moved on to pack up the loft area. I could hear the small talk between her and Charlie as they worked on packing the items I wanted to take with us. After being permanently released from the hospital two months ago, I'd been staying with Charlie and Marcus in a condo they'd bought. Since arriving that day in my hospital room when my brain decided to wake up and face the real world, both my sister and her fiancé had decided it was time to put down roots. They were in the process of opening a clinic in the city and were talking of adopting a child from the Congo once things settled down.

By "settled down," I knew they were referring to me.

It had been Nina who came up with an alternate living arrangement for me so that Charlie and Marcus could move on with their life.

"Hey, Diane? Are you sure you don't want to take your bed with you? It'll be more comfortable than Nina's spare bed; trust me on that," Charlie called out.

"I'll buy a new one; it's okay." The last thing I wanted was to sleep in a bed full of memories. Brian's ghost would always be there with me and I needed a clean break. I would never forget my husband, but I couldn't continue to think he was still only in London and soon to return home. No matter how much I wanted to.

I stared at the ultrasound in my hand and desperately tried to recall the feel of Grace in my arms, the real weight of her as I held her lifeless body in the hospital, not the memory of the doll that I'd carried around pretending was Grace. I wish I could remember those moments, those hours, those days, even if it meant reliving both her and Brian's death. I wanted nothing else more. But for some reason, those memories were gone.

The doctor said they could return, that one day I may see something that will trigger those hidden moments, but not to expect them. I wanted to, though, I really wanted to.

As hard as they would be, I welcomed the full reality of what happened to me. I couldn't hide from it; I refused to.

I grabbed some tissue paper and wrapped that ultrasound image before placing it in the box on the ground beside me. Later today Marcus would come and pack up the baby furniture and drop it off at the local women's shelter; tomorrow a local charity would pick up the other furniture and household items I didn't need.

Nina lived in a small cottage-type home just off the bay and she had graciously suggested that I move in with her. I loved being with Charlie and Marcus, but I knew I was holding them back from moving forward with their life, and since I considered Nina part of my family, I didn't hesitate to take her up on her offer.

I was taking baby steps back into the real world. I wasn't ready to return to work and Walter understood that. To be honest, I wasn't sure if I ever would be ready to return there. I'm not sure I could live that life again, be that woman who was in charge of a company. I had a hard enough time managing daily activities when left on my own. I didn't recognize who I was anymore but I knew that one day I would. Until then, as Nina continued to tell me, I needed only to focus on myself and my health. Everything else after that would fall into place.

"Don't forget, Marcello is saving a table for us tonight for dinner." Charlie stood behind me and reached for one of the stuffed teddy bears that lined the shelf above Grace's crib. She pointed to the box and I shook my head. I kept one stuffed animal of hers, one that Brian and I had picked out together. It was a little lion with the softest fur for a mane and even now, it melted my heart to hold it.

"Sounds good." When I started to get day-trips from the hospital, the one place I always wanted to go was to Marcello's restaurant. I'd sit in that little sitting area and watch the people around me. Marcello would always serve me some bruschetta and sparkling water and we'd chat for a little bit before he'd have to leave to greet other customers. Now that I was out for good, the four of us went out for dinner on a weekly basis.

"Are you doing okay?" Charlie reached for a little sleeper and folded it before laying it to the side.

"It's hard. I remember sitting in that rocker and singing Grace to sleep as if it happened yesterday. It's a memory I don't want to lose even though I know it's not real."

"I don't think you need to lose all of them, Dee. Every mother wants to remember the feel of their child in her arms. That's natural." Charlie folded another sleeper before she picked up a pile I'd sorted earlier and placed it in a plastic container labeled *Baby Clothing*.

I picked up a little dress Brian had bought. Toward the end, he would always surprise me with two items for the baby—one for a boy and one for a girl, just in case. I'd already packed the boy clothing, but took my time with the adorable girl clothing.

"This was one of the first outfits Brian bought for her." I held up the tiny yellow dress with pink embroidery for Charlie to see. "He was going to buy a tie to match the dress and wear it for a photo with her." I smiled at the memory of Brian's enthusiasm. He would have made such a wonderful father. My heart hitched in pain at the thought.

"Do you want to keep it?" Charlie placed her hand over mine and squeezed.

Did I want to keep it? Of course I did. I wanted to keep every outfit that I remembered placing on Grace. I wanted to keep every item that held a piece of memory. My eyes welled up with tears and I quickly shook my head.

"It's okay if you do," she whispered.

I folded up the dress in response and handed it to her to place in the container. I'd rather pack up a few items that I wanted to keep.

Charlie ignored me and placed the dress in the box beside me. "It was one of the first outfits he bought. You should keep it."

We worked in silence together, my sister and I, as we packed up the remainder of the nursery. In the end I kept more items than I had intended, but there were so many things I couldn't part with, not yet. One day, maybe. But my memories of Grace were still too real. I was having a hard time saying good-bye to my daughter.

When her room was all packed and both Nina and Charlie had gone downstairs to fill up the small rental trailer hooked up to Marcus's SUV, I sat down in the rocking chair I couldn't bear to take with me and opened the journal that contained the memories of the life I lived with Grace. I knew they weren't real. I knew that this had been a dream I'd lived, but they were still my memories and the only ones that I had of my daughter.

I read the first few lines, tears streaming down my face, and knew I had never written anything more real and more powerful than those first three sentences.

This was a perfect moment. In the silence, with the hint of dawn peeking through the curtains, where promises of a better day were offered.

I stared down at the twinkling blue eyes of my sweet darling baby and knew hope for the first time in a long, long time. Grace was everything I didn't deserve and everything I longed for. Just one look at her bow-shaped lips, wispy blond hair, and sweeping eyelashes, and I knew, from the moment I first saw her, that I could never go back to the way I used to be.

———

ACKNOWLEDGMENTS

Women are strong human beings. We carry the weight of the world on our shoulders (or so it feels). There was no way I could have written this story without the help of women who have experienced postpartum depression and psychosis. Daily, as stories were shared with me, I would marvel at the strength, determination, and love these women had. My heart goes out to each and every one of you—thank you, for sharing your stories with me. Women like you are my heroes.

I couldn't have written this story of a mother's love without the support of my own family. Jarrett, you were my inspiration for diving into the story of a couple in love, and my girls, you were my rays of sunshine when the emotional depth of what I was writing got to me. And Judah, thank you for always being there to help me plot out my scenes and for your awesome suggestions on how to make things better. Yes, if I add chocolate to any scene there's bound to be a little bit of happiness!

A special thank you to Ken Pelkman and Ron Aitken for letting me pick your brains when it came to IT queries—this girl's brain is meant for writing, not understanding the complexity of running an IT department or even knowing how to stop the swirling circle of despair on my computer. Thank you for your patience and for answering my multitude of questions.

Julie Alberts-Magnum, I loved your pickle story! Thank you for sharing it on my author page on Facebook—there's a section in here just for you!

I couldn't have written this story without the amazing team behind me at Lake Union Publishing, specifically Carmen Johnson and Helen Cattaneo. Carmen, your support has made this story into something more than I could have dreamed of. I'm thankful to have an editor like you!

While I wrote this, I lived through the devastating destruction of the Alberta Flood 2013. I believe I live in the best city in Canada as the residents of Calgary bonded together during this terrible time in a way I've never seen. On Twitter, Mookie Wilson (a.k.a. @mookalicious) was one of those Calgarians who went above and beyond his regular DJ persona and helped foster the spirit of the west in a way I've never seen. Thanks Mookie for letting me use one of your sayings—the context might be a bit different than intended, but nonetheless, it's there.

ABOUT THE AUTHOR

Steena Holmes grew up in a small town in Canada and holds a bachelor's degree in Theology. She is the author of *Finding Emma* and *Emma's Secret*. She has received the Indie Excellence Award and is a *USA Today* bestselling author. She lives in Calgary with her husband and three daughters and loves to wake up to the Rocky Mountains each morning.